STAR WARS™

GALACTIC ADVENTURES
STORYBOOK COLLECTION

Disney

LUCASFILM
PRESS

Los Angeles • New York

Collection © & TM 2018 Lucasfilm Ltd.

"Darth Maul and the Rathtars" adapted by Steve Behling and illustrated by TomatoFarm, based on *Star Wars: Darth Maul #1* by Cullen Bunn

"Size Matters Not" adapted by S. T. Bende and illustrated by TomatoFarm, based on *Star Wars #26* by Jason Aaron

"A Jedi's Control" adapted by S. T. Bende and illustrated by TomatoFarm, based on *Star Wars: Obi-Wan & Anakin #1* by Charles Soule

"Darth Vader and the Weapon of a Sith" adapted by Ivan Cohen and illustrated by TomatoFarm, based on *Star Wars: Darth Vader: Dark Lord of the Sith #3-5* by Charles Soule

"Leia Charts Her Own Course" adapted by Liz Marsham and illustrated by TomatoFarm, based on *Star Wars: Princess Leia #1* by Mark Waid

"Chewbacca and the Courageous Kid" adapted by Nate Millici and illustrated by Pilot Studio, based on *Star Wars: Chewbacca #1-3* by Gerry Duggan

"Luke and the Lost Jedi Temple" adapted by Jason Fry and illustrated by Pilot Studio, based on *Weapon of a Jedi* by Jason Fry

"Han and the Rebel Rescue" adapted by Nate Millici and illustrated by Pilot Studio, based on *Smuggler's Run* by Greg Rucka

"The Rebellion's Biggest Heist" adapted by Meredith Rusu and illustrated by TomatoFarm, based on *Star Wars #22-23* by Jason Aaron

"R2-D2 and the Renegade Rescue" adapted by Meredith Rusu and illustrated by TomatoFarm, based on *Star Wars #36* by Jason Aaron

"Lando's Big Score" adapted by Steve Behling and illustrated by TomatoFarm, based on *Star Wars: Lando #1-2* by Charles Soule

"Leia and the Great Island Escape" adapted by Jason Fry and illustrated Pilot Studio, based on *Moving Target* by Cecil Castelluci and Jason Fry

"Poe and the Missing Ship" adapted by Nate Millici and illustrated by Pilot Studio, based on *Before the Awakening* by Greg Rucka

"C-3PO's New Arm" adapted by Rebecca L. Schmidt and illustrated by TomatoFarm, based on *Star Wars: C-3PO #1* by James Robinson

"Rey's First Flight" adapted by Rebecca L. Schmidt and illustrated by TomatoFarm, based on *Before the Awakening* by Greg Rucka

"Stormtrooper in Training" adapted by Calliope Glass and illustrated by TomatoFarm, based on *Before the Awakening* by Greg Rucka

"Captain Phasma's Escape from Starkiller Base" adapted by Ivan Cohen and illustrated by TomatoFarm, based on *Star Wars: Captain Phasma #1* by Kelly Thompson

"Rose and Paige Fight for the Resistance" adapted by Calliope Glass and illustrated by TomatoFarm, based on *Cobalt Squadron* by Elizabeth Wein

Printed in the United States of America

First Edition, October 2018

10 9 8 7 6 5 4 3 2 1

FAC-038091-18241

Library of Congress control number on file

ISBN 978-1-368-00353-7

Visit the official *Star Wars* website at: www.starwars.com.

SUSTAINABLE FORESTRY INITIATIVE
Certified Sourcing
www.sfiprogram.org
SFI-00993
This Label Applies to Text Stock Only

CONTENTS

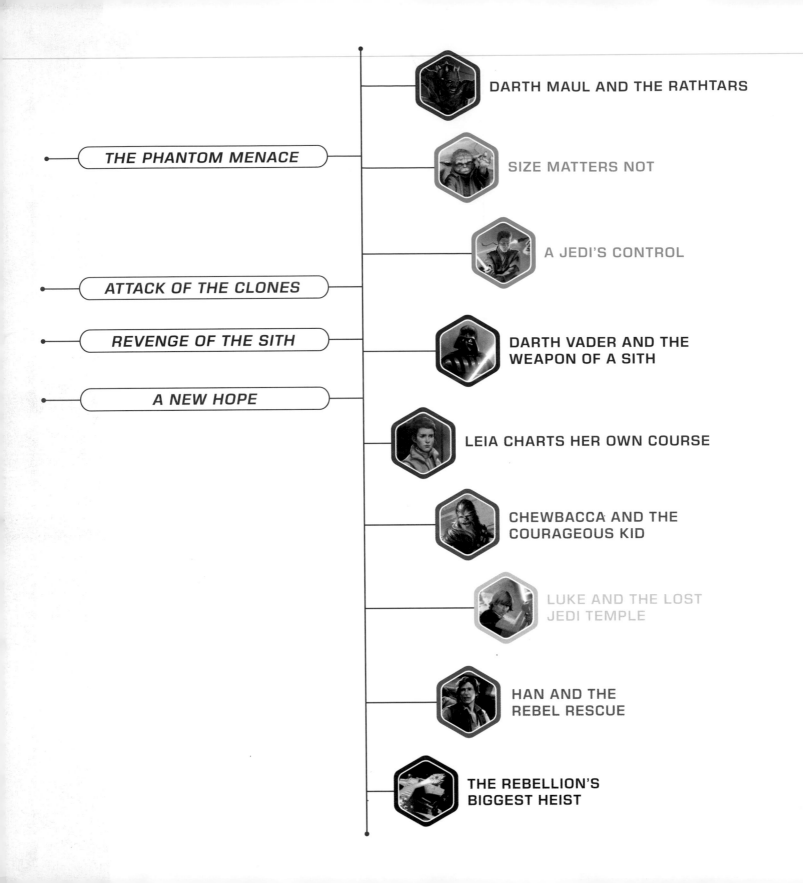

THE PHANTOM MENACE

ATTACK OF THE CLONES

REVENGE OF THE SITH

A NEW HOPE

DARTH MAUL AND THE RATHTARS

SIZE MATTERS NOT

A JEDI'S CONTROL

DARTH VADER AND THE WEAPON OF A SITH

LEIA CHARTS HER OWN COURSE

CHEWBACCA AND THE COURAGEOUS KID

LUKE AND THE LOST JEDI TEMPLE

HAN AND THE REBEL RESCUE

THE REBELLION'S BIGGEST HEIST

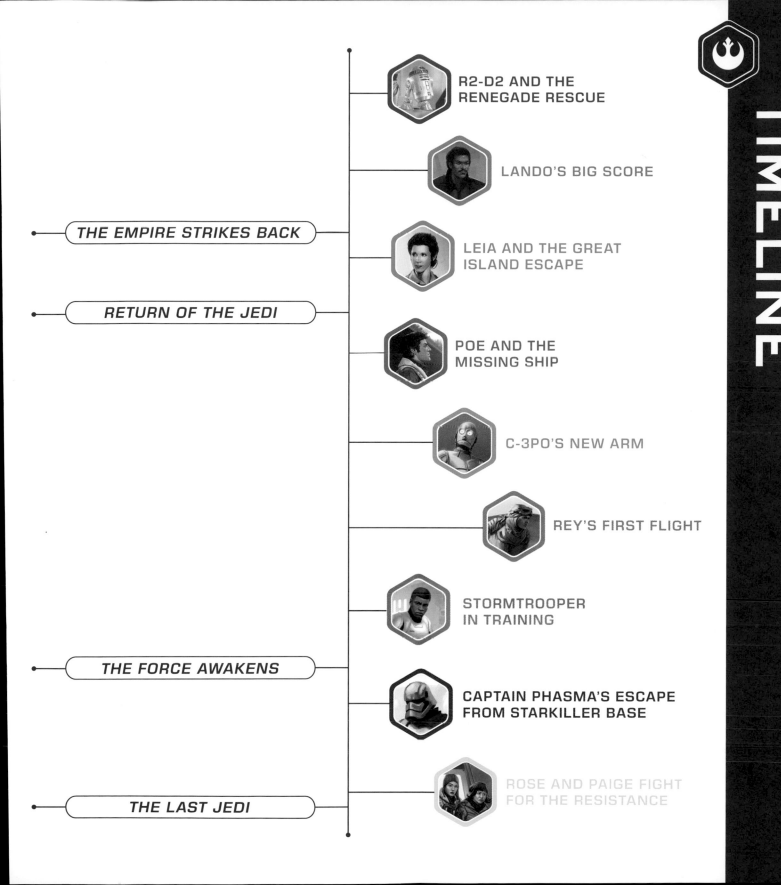

TIMELINE

R2-D2 AND THE
RENEGADE RESCUE

LANDO'S BIG SCORE

THE EMPIRE STRIKES BACK

LEIA AND THE GREAT
ISLAND ESCAPE

RETURN OF THE JEDI

POE AND THE
MISSING SHIP

C-3PO'S NEW ARM

REY'S FIRST FLIGHT

STORMTROOPER
IN TRAINING

THE FORCE AWAKENS

CAPTAIN PHASMA'S ESCAPE
FROM STARKILLER BASE

ROSE AND PAIGE FIGHT
FOR THE RESISTANCE

THE LAST JEDI

YODA

QUI-GON JINN

OBI-WAN KENOBI

MACE WINDU

ANAKIN SKYWALKER

SENATOR PALPATINE

R2-D2

C-3PO

LUKE SKYWALKER   PRINCESS LEIA   HAN SOLO

CHEWBACCA   LANDO CALRISSIAN   LOBOT

REY

FINN

POE DAMERON

BB-8

DARTH SIDIOUS

DARTH MAUL

DARTH VADER

ROSE TICO   PAIGE TICO   VICE ADMIRAL HOLDO

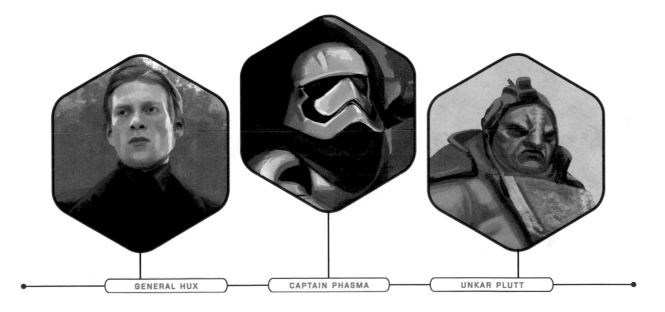

GENERAL HUX   CAPTAIN PHASMA   UNKAR PLUTT

A long time ago in a galaxy far, far away. . . .

THERE WASN'T MUCH TO DO ON THE JUNGLE PLANET TWON KETEE, unless you liked being eaten by rathtars.

Rathtars were deadly creatures, feared throughout the galaxy for their long powerful tentacles and rows on rows of sharp teeth.

But Darth Maul was not afraid of rathtars. In fact, he had traveled to the smelly swampy planet to face them and hone his fighting skills.

For years Darth Maul had been training in secret under the watchful eye of the evil Sith Lord Darth Sidious. The two dark warriors wanted to wipe out the Jedi Knights, the galaxy's guardians of peace and justice.

Skilled with a lightsaber and in the ways of the dark side of the Force, Darth Maul was always looking for a new challenge—something that would test his power.

So he decided to train against the fearsome rathtars while he waited for Darth Sidious to give him new orders. Maul knew he must be ready for the day when he would face the Jedi.

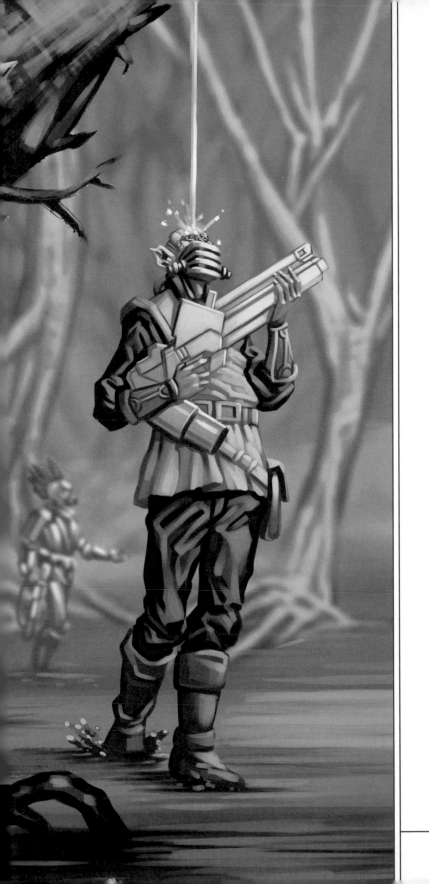

Darth Maul had hired a group of hunters to flush out the rathtars for him on Twon Ketee. The hunters didn't know who Darth Maul was, only that he had promised to pay them well.

Maul stayed behind the hunters, hidden in the shadow of a tree. He needed to focus. He needed to practice sensing danger before it appeared and staying quiet so his enemies didn't sense *him* until it was too late.

He quieted his mind and reached out using the dark side of the Force.

They are near.

The Sith felt the presence of the rathtars.

"Hey, fellas," said one hunter as he splashed through the swampy water, "do you smell something?"

The other hunters didn't smell anything. But one hunter *felt* something wet and slimy ooze onto the top of his head. . . .

Suddenly, there was a horrible screeching sound.

RRRREEEEEEAAOOOOOR!

The hunters looked up, and there it was—a vicious rathtar! The beast dropped from the tree above, its tentacles slashing everywhere. Disgusting green drool dripped

from the creature's big mouth full of razor-sharp teeth.

The hunters panicked. They had found the rathtar for their mysterious client. But where was he? They agreed to help *find* a rathtar . . . not fight it!

"I'm not getting paid enough for this!" said one of the hunters as they all scattered.

Then, from out of nowhere, Darth Maul appeared. He leapt right for the rathtar's gaping mouth!

Everyone in the galaxy knew just how dangerous a hungry rathtar could be. But did anyone yet know how dangerous Darth Maul could be?

The Sith used the terrible power of the dark side of the Force to guide his spear, and just as quickly as the battle had begun, it was over.

Darth Maul had defeated the rathtar!

But then he felt another disturbance in the Force. There was something else lurking nearby.

RRRREEEEEAAOOOOOR!

The Sith turned his head quickly and saw another rathtar drop from the trees.

Pack hunters.

Darth Maul wanted to use his two-bladed blood-red lightsaber. But he couldn't. If he used the lightsaber, any hunters who remained in the jungle would quickly realize that he was a Sith. And if anyone discovered that secret, Darth Sidious would be very angry.

The creature attacked Maul with great speed, but the Sith was faster and more agile. He quickly ducked under and leapt over the rathtar's tentacles, taking them out one by one with his spear.

The creature was growing impatient and let out a horrible roar as it tried to grab Maul and make him its next meal.

But the Sith simply jumped high in the air and hooked the end of his spear around one of the rathtar's tentacles, pulling hard.

The rathtar was hanging from a tree branch. Calling on the dark side of the Force and using all his strength, Darth Maul pulled on his spear as hard as he could. Soon the branch began to crack!

The branch broke, and *SPLASH!*—the rathtar fell into the murky green water below.

Darth Maul had defeated not one but two deadly rathtars, and he sensed that his training was nearly complete.

His trial over, Darth Maul left the defeated rathtars on Twon Ketee. He knew it was time to return to his master on the planet Coruscant. There, in secret, he met with Darth Sidious.

"These games could prove your undoing, my apprentice," said the evil Sith Lord. "You must be patient. For soon, we will strike."

Maul listened to his master. Rathtars were some of the most feared creatures in all the galaxy, and he had defeated them with ease.

So when the time came, Darth Maul was sure that he could do the same to the Jedi.

A LONG TIME AGO IN A GALAXY FAR,

far away, a brave group of men and women stood up for what was right. They were known as Jedi Knights, and they were guardians of peace and justice. They used wisdom to help those in need, carried elegant weapons called lightsabers, and received their power from the Force—an energy field created by all living things. When the dark side of the Force overpowered the light, it was up to the Jedi to restore the balance.

And one powerful Jedi flew in a silver starship toward the faraway planet of Botor to do just that.

For on Botor, a large fortress hid a horde of heavily armed pirates. The pirates earned their living by selling valuable items on the black market. Though they usually dealt in weapons and supplies, they had recently acquired something far more valuable—a prize that was sure to bring in their biggest payoff yet.

Crouched inside a metal cage was a young boy named Lo. Lo was perfectly ordinary in every way except one: he was able to move things just by looking at them. He didn't understand this power, and he didn't know that his gift was the

reason the pirates had captured him. He only knew that he was frightencd.

Lo shivered while two dozen menacing pirates gathered around his cage. The boy studied his captors' thick arms, pointed blasters, and cruel glares before turning his attention to the leader sitting atop a throne. This was Lord Alorg.

"Please," Lo whispered to the cloaked creature. "I don't know why I'm here."

Lord Alorg narrowed his eyes. "You're a Force user," he said. "And we all know what happens to Force users. Don't we?"

Suddenly, a guard ran into the lair. He warned the pirates that a ship had landed outside and they needed to be ready to fight.

Lord Alorg drummed long fingers against his throne. He had expected the Jedi to come for Lo. But Botor was Alorg's territory, and nobody took something from him without paying . . . not even the galaxy's most powerful protectors.

"Is it a Jedi?" A short pirate raised his blaster. "A *real* Jedi?"

The guard frowned. "I've never seen one before," he admitted. "But he's . . . definitely not what I expected."

Lord Alorg growled.

"Whoever he is, he'd better have our money if he wants the kid."

Lo's stomach lurched. As the doors of the fortress parted, he tried to steady himself on the floor of his cage. A bright beam of sunshine pierced the darkness, forcing Lo to close his eyes. When he opened them again, a brave Jedi was walking into the pirates' lair.

The pirates raised their weapons, preparing to fight a mighty Jedi warrior. But laughter burst from their throats as an aging green figure proceeded forward.

With his small size and unsteady steps, Yoda didn't look like a powerful Jedi. In fact, he didn't look like a Jedi at all!

Yoda stood quietly as the pirates' laughter echoed around him. He knew what the pirates could not understand—that a Jedi's strength flowed not from his or her size but from the Force itself.

"Find this humorous, I do not," Yoda warned.

"Heh." Lord Alorg looked down on Yoda. "What are you supposed to be, little fella?"

"The boy's escort to Coruscant, I am," Yoda said calmly, "where his training he will begin."

Alorg demanded payment, but Yoda shook his head.

"The Jedi care not for wealth," he said. "The Force is our only companion."

Lord Alorg sneered. "Then it looks like you and the Force just walked into a whole mess of trouble."

As Lo watched anxiously from his cage, Lord Alorg ordered his guards to attack Yoda. The Jedi refused to be intimidated by the towering, angry pirates. A youngling was trapped, and he would not abandon someone who needed help.

The guards lunged at Yoda, and the brave Jedi raised his palm. He used the Force to seize control of the pirates. Their hands balled into fists and their eyes widened in surprise. When Yoda twitched his fingers, the taller guard's arm shot forward to punch his partner in the face!

"Ow!" The shorter guard cried out as his partner hit him again. "Stop it!"

Yoda waited for Lord Alorg to call off his men. But instead of releasing Lo, Alorg ordered his guards to attack the boy. Yoda couldn't allow an innocent child to be harmed. The pirate lord's cruelty would cost him greatly.

The Jedi knew what he had to do.

Once more, Yoda told the guards to stop.

"Only more violence does violence create," he cautioned.

But the guards crept closer to Lo's cage, forcing Yoda to act. Lo watched with wide eyes as the small Jedi raised one hand and used the Force to slam the guards onto the ground without ever touching them.

The rest of the pirates charged Yoda, but the Jedi expertly deflected their attacks,

sending one, then the next hurtling across the room and onto the floor.

Finally, only Lord Alorg remained. The pirate leader leapt from his throne to tackle Yoda, but the Jedi sent him flying across the room. Lord Alorg hit the ground hard, landing beside a pile of guards. When the whole horde lay still, Yoda looked up in triumph. He had taken out an entire room of pirates!

With a slow breath, Yoda turned his attention to Lo. The Jedi calmly stepped around his fallen foes before reaching out to open Lo's cage. The door sprung open. Yoda had saved him. He was free!

Yoda offered his hand to Lo.

"Time to go, it is," he said kindly.

Lo's fingers shook as he reached up to grasp Yoda's palm. The Jedi guided him out of the cage and helped him to his feet. The two stepped across the piles of pirates, forging their path with cautious steps. When they reached the door, they emerged from the darkness to walk hand in hand into the light. As they stood in the sunshine, Yoda turned to Lo and spoke the words that would forever change his life.

"Begun, your training has."

Yoda took Lo to Jedi Knight Qui-Gon Jinn and his Padawan Obi-Wan Kenobi. They would escort Lo to his new home—the Jedi Temple.

"Worry not, Lo," Yoda assured the youngling. "Safe you will be with Qui-Gon Jinn."

Lo studied the two men. They were big and strong. Lo was small and scared, and he didn't understand how he could move things just by looking at them. But if there was one lesson he had learned from Yoda, it was that things weren't always what they seemed—and that even someone who was small could be very, very powerful.

Size mattered not.

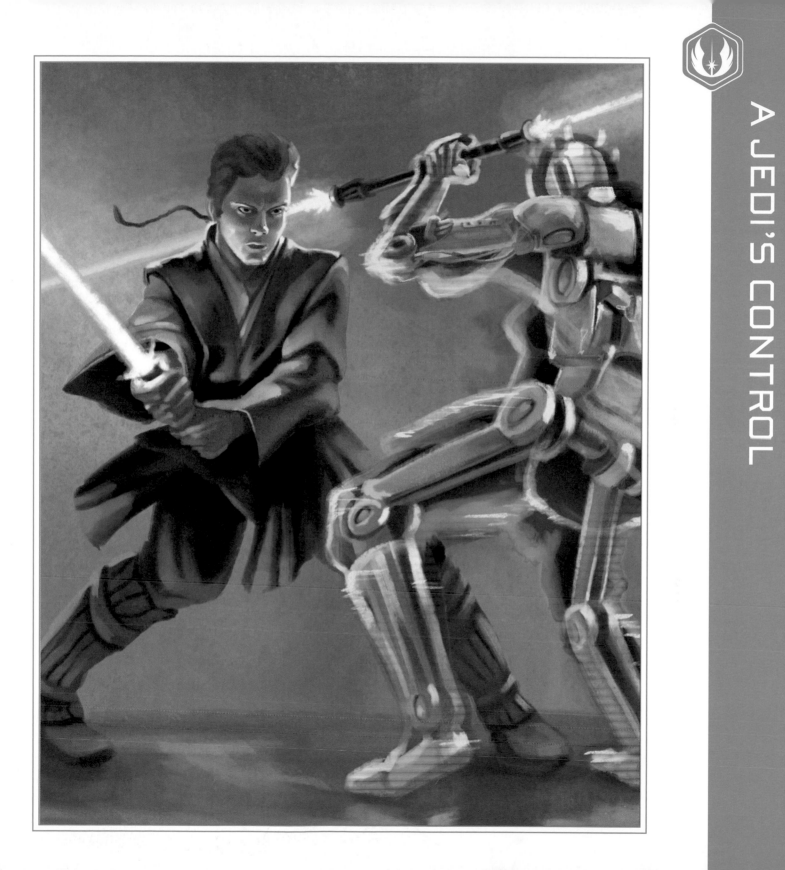

BECOMING A JEDI MEANT EVERYTHING

to Anakin Skywalker. Now that he was a Padawan learner, he lived in the Jedi Temple on Coruscant and dedicated his life to studying the ways of the Force.

Each morning, Anakin woke up early to meditate in his room, learn about the Force from his teachers, and practice using his lightsaber. He and his fellow Padawans worked tirelessly to master control over all aspects of their lives, from their emotions to their weapons.

Control was one of the most important skills for a Jedi to learn . . . but it was the one Anakin struggled with most.

One day, as Jedi Masters Obi-Wan Kenobi and Mace Windu oversaw the Padawans' lightsaber training, they were joined by a very important guest.

Chancellor Palpatine, the leader of the Galactic Senate, stood on the balcony with the Jedi Masters. The three men looked down as Anakin squared off against a training droid.

Though Anakin had been older than the rest of the Padawans when he had come to the temple for training, his natural talent and intense focus had quickly helped him catch up to his peers. He was an exceptionally skilled fighter—a fact that did not go unnoticed by the Chancellor.

"I see the boy has taken an interest in the lightsaber," Palpatine said.

He smiled as Anakin used one hand to force his opponent's weapon to the side.

With the droid at a disadvantage, Anakin spun around to attack from behind. He swung his lightsaber overhead, driving the droid back.

Anakin was in his element . . . but he was distracted by the Chancellor. Senators rarely came to the temple, and this particular politician was one Anakin really wanted to impress.

Since the Chancellor had already seen several Padawans fight a regulation droid, Anakin decided to battle a more advanced opponent—one who was sure to impress his teachers. He clicked a button on his belt and the droid instantly transformed into a far more sophisticated—and deadly—enemy.

Anakin's new opponent was a Nightbrother—a Force-sensitive Zabrak who had been raised on the planet Dathomir and trained to hurt others. The droid now bore the likeness of Darth Maul, the evil Sith whose double-bladed lightsaber had brought an end to the very Jedi who had freed Anakin from slavery and secured his place as a Padawan: Qui-Gon Jinn.

Anakin had heard from Obi-Wan the story of how Darth Maul had defeated Qui-Gon and how, once Qui-Gon fell, Obi-Wan had resumed the battle, channeling the Force and fighting the evil Sith with every ounce of his training.

Obi-Wan had been relentless in avenging his master, but Darth Maul had used the dark side of the Force to gain the advantage—pushing Obi-Wan over a ledge. Obi-Wan had grabbed on to the wall and clung on tight while his lightsaber tumbled down the seemingly bottomless shaft below. He had been trapped!

But Obi-Wan had then calmed his mind, drawn on the Force, and called Qui-Gon's lightsaber to him as he leapt from the pit, striking Darth Maul across the waist to end the battle.

Once Darth Maul was gone, Obi-Wan had dropped to his knees and vowed to honor his master's legacy by training young Anakin Skywalker.

Now Obi-Wan watched with wide eyes as Anakin battled a hologram of his fallen foe, re-creating Obi-Wan's maneuvers.

"Anakin has been asking me about my fight with the Sith," he explained to Mace Windu. "Very detailed questions."

Anakin lunged forward. With his lightsaber he struck the training droid across the waist, destroying his opponent and winning the battle in a move that was all too familiar to his master.

Obi-Wan drew a sharp breath.

"I had no idea he would . . ."

Mace Windu shook his head, concerned about the boy's level of interest in the fallen Sith, but Chancellor Palpatine smiled.

"A boy of his age, altering a training droid? That is more than unexpected. I would call that . . . impressive."

The Chancellor may have been impressed, but Anakin's fellow Padawans were not. Whispers filled the arena as Anakin deactivated his lightsaber and wiped the sweat from his brow.

"He may be good with a lightsaber," a brown-haired boy murmured, "but that doesn't mean he'll make a good Jedi."

"No," another agreed. "After all, he's just a slave to his emotions."

"Exactly. Just a slave . . ."

Hurt twisted in Anakin's gut. He had grown up as a slave on Tatooine, but he'd worked hard to earn the respect of his teachers and his place within the Jedi Order.

If the Padawans thought he didn't belong, he would have to show them just how well he could control emotions . . . *their* emotions.

Anakin raised one arm toward the boys.

"What are you feeling now?" he shouted as he drew on the Force.

With a twist of Anakin's hand, the Padawans' lightsabers flew from their grasp, landing squarely in Anakin's outstretched palm. The boys cried out in surprise, but Anakin held tight to their weapons, breathing heavily as anger coursed through him.

"Anakin!"

Obi-Wan leapt from the balcony. He stood over Anakin in the arena.

"Enough!"

Anakin bowed his head as reason caught up to him. He had disappointed Obi-Wan and proven the boys right. He *had* let his emotions control him, and he was upset with himself.

"I didn't mean to frighten you." Anakin returned the boys' weapons. "You're right, I do need better control of my emotions. Please, accept my apology."

"Of course," the taller boy said, shaken. "Forget it."

The two Padawans returned to their training while Anakin hung his head in frustration. He still had so much to learn.

Chancellor Palpatine had watched the exchange with interest. Anakin's training was far from complete . . . and Palpatine wanted to be the one to teach him.

"Send him to me," he offered to Mace Windu. "I may be able to help."

Nobody noticed the calculating gleam in the Chancellor's eyes. Anakin Skywalker's inability to control his feelings may have been a weakness for a Jedi, but the Chancellor had a very different path in mind for the boy.

On that path, Anakin's emotions would prove to be his greatest strength . . . and the Chancellor's most powerful weapon.

DARTH VADER PILOTED HIS SHIP THROUGH THE UPPER ATMOSPHERE OF AL'DOLEEM.

Once a promising Jedi Knight known as Anakin Skywalker, the young man had surrendered to the dark side of the Force and become Darth Vader. But he had lost his lightsaber during a duel with his former friend and teacher Obi-Wan Kenobi.

Now the evil Sith Lord Darth Sidious had challenged his new apprentice to construct his own lightsaber.

But in order for him to do so, Vader had to first find a Jedi with a lightsaber, and that would be no easy task. Darth Sidious had used his clone army to destroy the Jedi Order.

However, Vader had heard of a Jedi Master named Kirak Infil'a who had escaped Darth Sidious's deadly attack.

So the Sith Lord had charted a course to the Jedi's home moon.

But as Vader prepared to land, Infil'a must have sensed his presence. . . .

Suddenly, a large, strange piece of metal struck the Sith's ship!

Infil'a had used the Force to fling a sculpture from below as a first line of defense.

A talented pilot, Vader was able to land his ship in spite of the damage.

He sensed Infil'a nearby, and he would not keep the Jedi waiting.

Vader needed to defeat the Jedi and take his lightsaber so he could return to Darth Sidious and finish his training.

Vader set out to find Infil'a. But before long, the Jedi launched a surprise attack, raising a heavy wall to trap the Sith in a canyon!

"You stink of darkness!" Infil'a bellowed from above.

Vader's anger flared. He did not have time for a discussion. He called on the dark side of the Force to reach up from the depth of the canyon to attack the Jedi.

With great effort, the Jedi broke free of Vader's Force grip.

"You will not defeat me that way," Infil'a boomed, activating his lightsaber. "You will not defeat me at all."

The Jedi sensed why Vader was there, and he had no intention of giving up his sacred weapon—especially not to a Sith, who would take control of the kyber crystal inside the lightsaber and turn it red, the mark of the dark side.

Infil'a called a wave of water down on Vader. The water flooded the canyon, pinning Vader in a deep undercurrent.

But Vader was stronger in the Force than Infil'a had thought.

With every ounce of his concentration, the Sith pushed the water to either side, clearing a path so he could climb to higher ground and go after the Jedi.

As Vader reached a bridge, he heard the sound of heavy wings beating down from above.

Five deadly raptorans circled the Sith, taking turns striking at their prey!

Vader used the Force to protect himself, slamming the flying creatures into the rocky walls of the mountainside.

The Jedi was surprised by Vader's strength.

He called off the raptorans' attack.

It was time for Infil'a to face the Sith himself.

As Vader climbed the mountain to confront Infil'a, he found the Jedi's servant droid instead. The droid wanted to protect his master.

But the loyal servant was no match for the dark side, and the Sith soon disabled him, taking the droid's glowing electro sword for himself.

Now nothing stood between Vader and Infil'a, but the Jedi was ready for him.

The two enemies battled hard at the edge of a cliff, equally matched in opposite sides of the Force.

Infil'a was determined not only to defeat Vader but to destroy the Sith Lord who had sent him.

"I will seek out your master and destroy him as well," said the Jedi between blows. "And then, I will restore the light of the Jedi to the galaxy."

With that, Infil'a used the Force to send Vader tumbling off the edge of the cliff!

Infil'a made his way to a nearby town to get his ship and go after Darth Sidious. But Vader—whose armor had saved him from his fall—was soon close behind.

He had realized something important: Infil'a had a weakness that Vader could use to defeat the Jedi.

There was something Infil'a cared about more than winning.

The Jedi cared about others.

The warriors faced off once more at the top of the city dam.

Infil'a was amazed to see Vader had survived the fall, and he was eager to defeat the Sith once and for all.

But then Vader set his final plan in motion, using the Force to rip the dam open and unleash a flood that spilled over the town.

While Infil'a desperately tried to repair the damage and save the city, Vader struck the winning blow, using the Force to steal the Jedi's lightsaber as Infil'a fell into the crashing waves.

Darth Vader returned to his new teacher, lightsaber in hand.

Darth Sidious was pleased with his young apprentice.

The Sith had defeated Infil'a, and he had used the dark side of the Force to turn the Jedi's green saber a deep red.

Darth Vader was ready to complete his training as a Sith at Sidious's side.

Together they would become more powerful than anyone could imagine.

THE REBELLION HAD WON A HUGE BATTLE.

Using information that Princess Leia Organa stole for them, the rebels had destroyed the evil Empire's most powerful weapon, the Death Star. But it was too late for Leia's homeworld, Alderaan. Before the battle, the Empire had used the Death Star to destroy the entire planet. Princess Leia was devastated. But she knew she needed to continue fighting with the Rebellion if there was any hope of defeating the evil Empire once and for all.

During the medal ceremony where Leia honored the other heroes of the battle,
Luke Skywalker, Han Solo, and Chewbacca the Wookiee, General Dodonna
reminded the Rebellion that their fight was far from over.

"The Empire is still strong, and we are in danger," he said. "There is a lot of work to do. You have all been given your jobs."

Leia looked over at him, puzzled. No one had given *her* a job yet.

After the ceremony, Leia went to speak with General Dodonna. She asked him to give her a new mission. The general told her that the best thing she could do for the Rebellion was stay hidden. The Empire was looking for her, and it was too dangerous to send her out.

Leia was upset. She didn't want to hide.

When Leia left the meeting with Dodonna, she was frustrated and distracted by her own thoughts.

Why couldn't she keep fighting for the Rebellion?

Suddenly, she bumped into an Alderaanian pilot named Evaan.

Leia was glad to meet someone else from her home planet, but Evaan had terrible news.

"The Empire is hunting down all remaining Alderaanians," she explained.

Leia couldn't believe her ears.

The Empire had already destroyed her home planet. Now they wanted to search the galaxy to capture her fellow Alderaanians? Leia wouldn't stand for it.

"I know what we must do," she said.

"'*We*'?" asked Evaan.

That night, Dodonna woke up in his room to see a hologram message playing. It was Leia!

"I am sending you this out of respect," said the hologram, "and to beg your understanding. It is my duty to gather the people of Alderaan who were not on the planet when it was destroyed. It is my duty to protect them from the Empire."

If Dodonna wouldn't let Leia fight for the Rebellion, she would fight for her people instead.

General Dodonna was furious, but it was too late. Leia, Evaan, and the droid R2-D2 were heading through space in a shuttle.

Before they could jump to hyperspace, Evaan noticed something on her radar.

"We're being pursued," said Evaan.

Two X-wings were chasing the shuttle and catching up fast. Dodonna had sent two rebel pilots to bring Leia back.

The speedy X-wings flew past the shuttle, then settled in front of it and started to slow down.

"What are they doing?" asked Leia.

"They're stopping us by getting in our way," replied Evaan. "We can't jump to hyperspace without hitting them."

Evaan tried to maneuver around the other pilots, but the X-wings were too fast. She would have to try another tactic. . . .

KLANG! The shuttle banged into one of the X-wings. A small metal piece flew off the shuttle and floated away into space. The shuttle started to wobble.

"That was a piece of our hyperdrive," said Evaan. "We can only fix it back at port."

"You did that on purpose!" said Leia. "You don't want me to put myself in danger. You want this mission to fail!"

The two rebel pilots heard Evaan and Leia over their comms. They pulled their X-wings back to give the shuttle more room.

"They're falling back," Evaan said.

"So what?" snapped Leia.

"So *this*," said Evaan, and pushed down the hyperdrive lever.

FWOOSH! The shuttle jumped to hyperspace and escaped.

Leia was confused. "I thought the hyperdrive was—"

"I wanted *them* to think that," explained Evaan. "The piece that flew away was a fake. Artoo and I figured out a plan, but we couldn't tell you without them hearing."

"Evaan, you are magnificent!" Leia shouted. "You too, Artoo!"

She knew her mission was important, and she would have been willing to do it alone. But it was nice having friends to help her.

The shuttle flew on through hyperspace, toward a galaxy full of people from Alderaan who needed Leia's help. Leia would honor her lost planet in her own way—by working and fighting and never giving up.

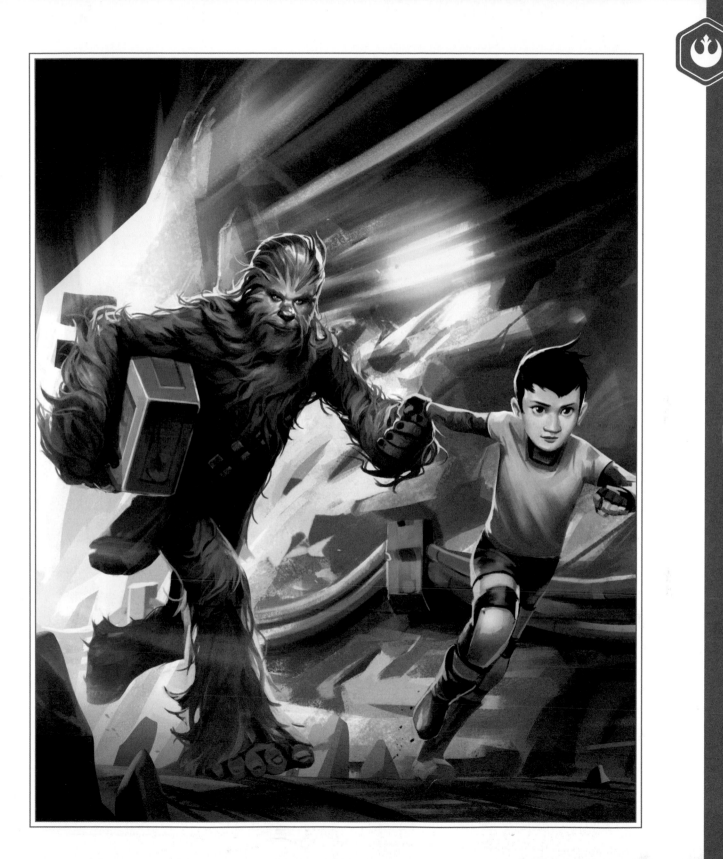

CHEWBACCA THE WOOKIEE WAS ON A MISSION.

He had helped the Rebellion destroy the Empire's dreaded superweapon, the Death Star, and his friends Han, Luke, and Leia needed his help to continue their fight to save the galaxy, but that would have to wait.

Chewbacca had something else he needed to take care of first.

Unfortunately, the ship Chewbacca had borrowed wasn't working properly.

He would need to fix the flight stabilizer to continue on his journey. So the Wookiee set out for a nearby village to find the part he needed.

When Chewbacca reached the local scrapyard, he overheard the manager, a gruff-looking Besalisk, giving a young girl a hard time about the speeder bike she was trying to sell.

"No sale! I know you stole this from Jaum," barked the Besalisk. "I bet he'd be more interested in having *you* back than the bike."

Chewbacca respected his fellow smugglers, and he didn't like the look of the electro-stun prod that the manager twisted in his grip, so the Wookiee stepped in just in time for the girl to escape.

With a new flight stabilizer in hand, Chewbacca made his way back to his ship, but he soon sensed that he was being followed.

It was the girl from the scrapyard. Her name was Zarro.

"I need some help," said the girl. "My dad and some of our friends are in big trouble."

Chewbacca roared.

"You don't have a translator?" Zarro asked.

Chewbacca roared again.

"Do you have a name?"

Chewbacca roared a third time.

Zarro was puzzled. "I don't know how to say that. . . ."

Zarro would not leave Chewbacca alone.

While he worked on fixing his ship, she told him why she needed his help.

Jaum, whose speeder bike she had stolen, was a gangster who had captured her and her father, along with many others, and forced them to work in one of his mines.

Zarro's dad had helped her escape with the bike, but she needed to go back to the mine to rescue him and the others. And she couldn't go alone.

Chewie groaned. His own mission would have to wait.

Back at the entrance to Jaum's mine, Zarro showed Chewie an air vent she needed him to climb down. The Wookiee was not pleased about the idea of shinnying down a tight air vent, but it was the only way for him to sneak inside without being detected.

Zarro had the opposite task. She needed to be detected so she could be thrown back into the mine.

Zarro was relieved to see her father again, but then Jaum arrived.

The gangster announced that he was selling the mine, and all the workers trapped inside, to the Empire! Zarro and her dad were doomed.

Suddenly, Chewbacca broke through the crumbling rocks above!

He had made his way down the cramped air vent and was able to battle Jaum's guards below.

But the gangster managed to flee in all the chaos.

Chewbacca, Zarro, and her father were okay, but they knew Jaum would soon send a fresh wave of guards, or something much worse, down to the mine. Chewie had his bowcaster, but they would need a weapon with more firepower if they were going to battle their way to freedom.

That's when the Wookiee spotted a little gonk droid nearby and quickly got to work.

Zarro had no idea what Chewbacca was doing . . .

. . . but she knew he needed to do it quickly.

A rumble tore through the mine.

It was a two-wheeled battle droid firing heavy plasma bolts!

BZZZACKK!

Chewbacca thrust a staff at the battle droid, and it fizzled to a stop.

He had rewired the gonk droid and connected its power source to the staff. Chewie had an electro-stun prod of his own!

With all the guards and battle droids out of the way, Chewbacca was able to make his way out of the mine through the main entrance. He wanted to make sure the coast was clear before Zarro and the rest of the workers escaped.

But Jaum and his last guard had set a trap!

The mine exploded in a fiery blast as Jaum's ship zoomed away from the planet.

The evil gangster had gotten away . . .

. . . but Chewbacca had saved the day!

It was a struggle, but the Wookiee managed to hold up part of the mine so everyone could run away from the collapsing rock.

With the entrance to the mine blocked by rubble, Zarro and her father and the workers needed to find another way out.

But they soon spotted something else to worry about: poisonous beetles were crawling their way!

"Don't step on them," Zarro's father explained. "That sends the swarm into a fury."

"We gotta move!" Zarro said.

"But slowly," her father added. "If we disturb them at all, they'll attack."

Chewie knew that firing his bowcaster at the beetles would probably qualify as "disturbing" them, but he didn't have a choice.

A river of beetles had started to swarm behind them. *FWINNG!*

The Wookiee fired a well-aimed blast at the ceiling of the mine behind them, causing a cascade of rocks to crumble on top of the beetles so the workers could run to safety.

Zarro and the other workers argued about how to escape the mine, but Chewie knew the only way out was up.

It was risky. Picking at the rocks above could cause the ceiling to collapse, as it had with the beetles. But it was their only option. And Chewbacca was the only one strong enough to try it.

Chewie grabbed a mining shovel and a long rope and started climbing.

It was hard work, slowly, carefully chipping away at the dirt and the rock while holding himself up. Chewbacca didn't like how often he was finding himself wriggling through such tight spaces . . .

. . . and he was glad when it was over!

Safely outside the mine, Chewie dropped the rope through the passageway he had created and pulled up Zarro, her father, and each of the other workers one by one.

"I'll never be able to thank you for keeping her safe and rescuing us," Zarro's father told Chewbacca as the girl gave the Wookiee one last hug.

Chewbacca simply roared a friendly good-bye.

Chewie returned to his ship and zoomed off into the stars.
He had helped Zarro complete her mission, and now he had to finish his own. . . .

The galaxy needed Chewbacca.
He had to return to his friends in the Rebellion to keep fighting the Empire.
But first he wanted to see his family.
That was the most important mission of all.

LUKE SKYWALKER WAS IN TROUBLE!

His Y-wing fighter had been damaged in a battle with the Empire, and he needed to find a safe place to land.

As he flew low over the jungle planet of Devaron, something interesting caught his eye. It was the ruins of a temple. The mysterious energy field known as the Force told him the temple was important.

Luke was traveling with his faithful droids, C-3PO and R2-D2. C-3PO feared Imperial stormtroopers would be waiting for them wherever they landed. But Luke sensed that he needed to visit the ruins.

Once on the ground, there was no sign of Imperial troops. A mechanic named Kivas and his daughter, Farnay, agreed to fix Luke's fighter while he and the droids explored.

The nearby village was bustling with life.

Luke soon found guides who were eager to take him hunting for creatures called pikhrons. But Luke didn't want to go hunting. He wanted to visit the Jedi temple.

The locals refused to help him. They said the temple was forbidden.

Only one guide would take Luke into the jungle. He was an alien named Sarco Plank. Farnay warned Luke that people who traveled with Sarco didn't return. Luke appreciated Farnay's warning, but he had no choice. The Force was calling him to the temple.

Sarco, Luke, and the droids mounted beasts called happabores and rode off into the jungle. On their journey Sarco noticed Luke's lightsaber—the weapon of a Jedi Knight. Luke didn't want Sarco to know he could feel the Force, so he pretended that he didn't know how to use the lightsaber.

When they reached the temple, R2-D2 detected Imperial probe droids floating among the ruins. The Empire clearly didn't want visitors.

Through the Force, Luke sensed a secret cave high on a cliff above an old riverbed. That would be their way in!

Leaving Sarco behind, Luke and the droids climbed into the cave and walked down a dark, twisty passageway.

When Luke reached the temple, he found it in ruins. Statues of ancient Jedi were scattered in pieces on the ground. But at it's center, Luke found a battered but beautiful courtyard. He heard a voice inside his head. It was his old teacher, Obi-Wan Kenobi!

Obi-Wan had taught Luke a little about the Force before the evil Darth Vader struck him down in a lightsaber duel. Obi-Wan was gone but could still speak to Luke through the Force. He told Luke that the Force had guided him to the temple. There Luke would learn to open his mind to the Force's teachings.

Luke took in his surroundings.

At the top of a nearby pillar was a lever. Luke tried and tried to use the Force to move it, but it wouldn't budge. He didn't know what to do.

Then a beautiful, brightly colored insect landed on Luke's arm. He heard Obi-Wan's voice again, urging him to feel the Force everywhere.

Through the Force, Luke focused on the lever once more, and it moved!

A metal orb emerged from the pillar. It was like the remote that Obi-Wan had once used to train Luke. Luke ignited his lightsaber and tried to command the Force. C-3PO and R2-D2 stood by, watching Luke as he dueled with the device that zipped through the air and fired stinging laser beams.

When the orb backed away, Luke smiled. He had passed the test.

Then two more remotes emerged! It was impossible to keep track of three devices at once! Luke almost felt like he'd be better off fighting blind, the way Obi-Wan made him train aboard the *Millennium Falcon*.

Luke realized that Obi-Wan had been trying to teach him to trust the Force

instead of his senses. Jedi Knights didn't guide the Force but let it guide *them*.

Luke took a deep breath and tried again. This time, he let the Force direct his movements.

The three training remotes flew into attack mode. Luke spun left and right, his lightsaber flashing. He fought for hours, and not one laser bolt got through his defenses!

Suddenly, a laser blast knocked Luke off his feet! But it wasn't a remote shooting at him. The Empire's stormtroopers had found him, and they had captured Farnay! She must have followed him to keep an eye on Sarco.

Luke was outnumbered and about to surrender when Sarco Plank emerged from behind the ruins. The guide was holding a crackling electrostaff and was there to help Luke!

Fighting side by side, Luke and Sarco defeated the Imperial soldiers.
But just as the last stormtrooper fell . . .

. . . Sarco turned on Luke and Farnay. He was much more dangerous than Luke had realized. Sarco was planning to steal Luke's lightsaber, melt down the droids, and loot any Jedi treasures left in the temple.

Sarco threw a grenade into the air, and it exploded with a brilliant flash and a thunderclap. The impact knocked Luke down and left him unable to see or hear.

Luke tried to fight Sarco, but he was facing the wrong way. As Farnay and the droids watched in horror, Sarco raised his electrostaff and walked slowly toward Luke.

Luke started to panic, but then he heard Obi-Wan's voice, reminding him that while his eyes and ears could deceive him, the Force was all-seeing.

Moving with incredible speed and using the Force to guide him, Luke spun into action! He swung the blade of his lightsaber into Sarco's chest, knocking the alien back. Sarco staggered and fell into a deep pit in the courtyard. Luke had defeated him for now, but the alien would surely rise again.

Farnay and the droids rushed over to Luke, but there was no time to celebrate. TIE fighters shrieked overhead. Luke, Farnay, and the droids knew they had to flee. Luke stopped for a moment in the ruins of the lost Jedi temple. Lifting his lightsaber, Luke swore he would become a Jedi Knight . . . perhaps even the greatest Jedi of all!

HAN SOLO AND CHEWBACCA WERE ON A SECRET MISSION FOR THE REBELLION.

A rebel spy named Lieutenant Ematt was stranded on a planet called Cyrkon in the Outer Rim. Ematt held top-secret information for the rebels, and it was imperative that Han and Chewie find him before the Empire did.

Han had not wanted to help with the mission. He was tired of sticking out his neck for the Rebellion. But Princess Leia knew that only Han and Chewie's ship, the *Millennium Falcon*, was fast enough to reach Cyrkon in time to save Ematt.

Han and Chewie touched down in one of the landing bays and set the engines to standby. Han had a feeling they would need to leave in a hurry.

Before Han and Chewie could even start their search for Ematt, they were surrounded by four bounty hunters!

Han owed money to the vilest gangster in the galaxy, Jabba the Hutt, and the slimy monster had grown impatient for his credits.

Jabba had hired a droid bounty hunter and his three companions to find Han.

Han and Chewie were trapped!

Then, just when Han and Chewie thought things couldn't get worse, a squad of Imperial stormtroopers started marching their way!

But Han had an idea. He shouted at the troopers that the bounty hunters were rebels!

The stormtroopers turned on the bounty hunters, eager to catch any rebel who might be searching for the missing Ematt.

In all the chaos, Han and Chewie managed to slip away unnoticed!

The Wookiee growled with relief.

Han and Chewie weaved their way through the busy marketplace to a cantina where Han knew he could get information about Ematt's location.

But this cantina was unlike any other. It was inside the cargo hold of a ship called the *Miss Fortune*.

Han greeted a woman with red hair. Her name was Delia, and she owned the cantina.

Sure enough, Delia knew where Ematt was hiding. She was surprised to see Han Solo on a mission for the rebels, but then again, Han was always full of surprises.

Han and Chewie rented a speeder and raced across the city. They needed to reach Ematt right away.

When they reached the hotel where Delia had told them Ematt was hiding, Han was
relieved to find that the rebel was okay.
Ematt was unsure of his rescuers, but there was no time for questions.

The bounty hunters had tracked them to the hotel!

Han, Chewie, and Ematt battled their way through the building and back to the speeder.

They were almost home free! Han could feel it. They just needed to get back to the *Falcon*.

Of course, nothing ever went quite as planned.

When Han, Chewie, and Ematt reached the landing bay, they ran right into a squad of stormtroopers! The Empire had been waiting for them.

Han's lies had only gotten them so far. The Imperials realized that Chewie and Han, not the bounty hunters, were the *real* rebels. And they were going to take them and Ematt away.

But Han had an idea, and all it took was a wink at Chewie for the Wookiee to catch on.

Chewbacca shoved Han into a pack of stormtroopers. The smuggler flailed, taking down as many troopers as he could.

The diversion worked. Chaos erupted!

Han pulled his blaster and fired at the generators along the perimeter of the landing bay. Explosions knocked the troopers off their feet!

Han noticed a familiar ship lining up a shot from above. It was the *Miss Fortune*! Delia sent down blasts to keep the troopers at bay while Han, Chewie, and Ematt boarded the *Falcon* and prepared for takeoff. Han had been right: they really *did* need to leave in a hurry!

The *Falcon* roared away from the polluted planet and joined the *Miss Fortune* in space. An Imperial Star Destroyer was waiting for them, along with a fleet of TIE fighters whizzing this way and that, pelting space with bright green blasts. The Empire was desperate to stop the rebels at any cost!

The Star Destroyer was edging closer, aiming to trap the rebel ships in its tractor beam. Running interference and dodging Imperial blasts, Han and Chewie pushed the *Falcon* to its limits to protect Delia.

After Han saw that the *Miss Fortune* had disappeared into the safety of unknown space, the *Millennium Falcon* jumped to lightspeed—at the last possible second before the Imperial tractor beam could latch on!

Han and Chewie had completed their mission for the Rebellion.
They may have been an unlikely pair of rebels, but they were rebels all the same!

DEEP IN SPACE, A BATTLE RAGED BETWEEN THE REBELS AND THE EMPIRE. But this wasn't just

any battle. The rebels were attacking a
massive Star Destroyer!

Luke Skywalker, Princess Leia, Han
Solo, and Chewbacca desperately needed
a large ship to deliver supplies to the
Rebellion's secret bases. The only ship
large enough for the job was an Imperial
Star Destroyer . . . which meant the rebels
needed to *steal* one from the Empire.

So they'd come up with a plan: a very
sneaky, dangerous, and *crazy* plan. But
the Rebellion trusted Luke, Leia, Han, and
Chewie. Somehow, the friends had a way
of making even the craziest plans in the
galaxy work.

146

The first thing the rebels needed to do was blast a hole in the side of the
Star Destroyer.

Han contacted the fleet.

"Red Squadron, this is the *Falcon*. We're making another run at it."

"These are our last proton bombs," Leia told him. "So we'd better make
them count."

"I can't believe I let you talk me into this," Han muttered. He had only recently
joined the Rebellion, so he was not used to fighting against powerful Imperial
battleships.

TIE fighters, protecting the Star Destroyer, fired at the *Millennium Falcon*. Han swerved to the left.

"Hold the ship steady, Han!" cried Leia.

"Sorry, I couldn't hear you because I'm too busy *saving our lives*!" Han shouted back.

More TIE fighters swarmed. Han swerved to the right.

Leia was waiting until just the right moment to drop the bombs on the Star Destroyer.

"We're out of time!" Han exclaimed. "You have to make the shot—now!"

"Bombs away!" Leia called.

BLAST!

It was a direct hit!

"Damage report!" cried the admiral of the Star Destroyer.

"The hull is breached," a crew member responded. "In sector nineteen-A."

"Nineteen-A?" The admiral gasped. "But that's near the main reactor engine!"

The admiral contacted his troops.

"Seal that hole! We cannot let the rebels fire upon the reactor!"

Out in space, a rebel pilot named Wedge started the second phase of their plan.

"I'm under heavy fire," he called over his comm. "Cover me while I make my run."

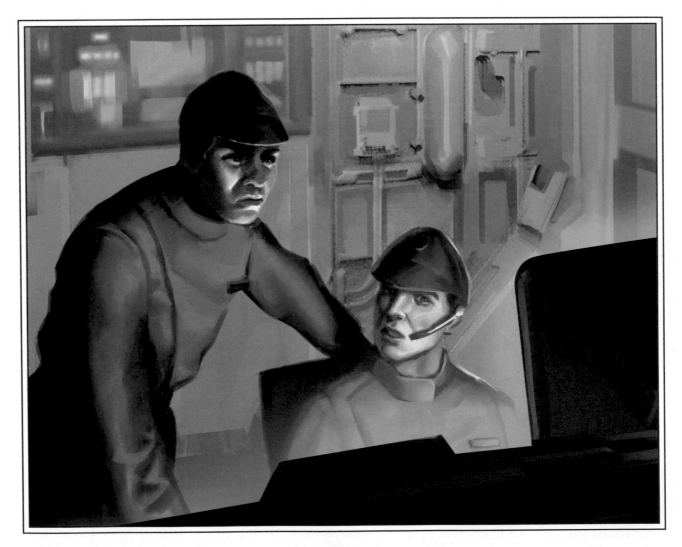

"I've got your back, Wedge," said Luke. He blasted two TIE fighters zeroing in on his friend. "And you've got this—good luck!"

Wedge zoomed his X-wing straight toward the hole the *Falcon* had made in the Star Destroyer.

Zap! Zap! Zap!

"Torpedoes are in!" he announced. "I repeat, torpedoes are in!"

The rebels watched . . . but nothing happened.

"We should see signs of the reactor overload by now," Han said. "The torpedoes must not have hit their mark."

"There are too many TIE fighters," another rebel pilot chimed in. "We're being overpowered."

"We have to end this," said Leia. "Or we'll all be captured."

"*I* have to end this," Luke said. "There's only one way to find out if the reactor was hit for sure. I'm going in!"

"Luke!" shouted Han and Leia. "What are you doing?"

But Luke didn't listen. He flew his X-wing straight *into* the hole in the Star Destroyer!

When he reached the reactor, he saw that the torpedoes *had* hit their mark—and the reactor was crackling with flames and energy sparks.

"It's been hit!" Luke informed his friends. "It's going to blow!"

"Admiral! The reactor is overloading," an Imperial crew member reported. "We only have seven minutes until destruction."

"How should we proceed?" another crew member asked.

The admiral looked around in shock. There was only one option.

"Abandon ship!" he commanded.

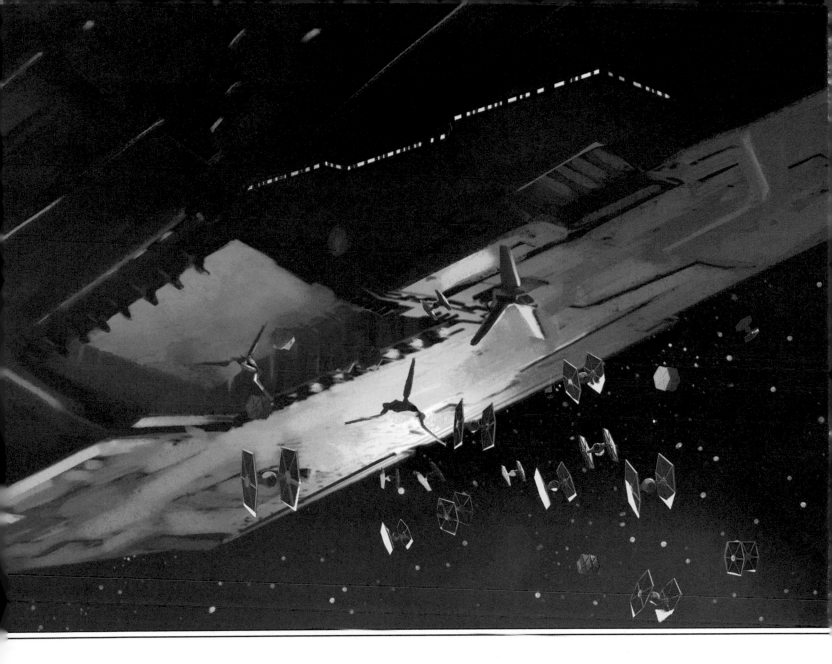

The Imperial troops immediately began to evacuate.

But in all the chaos of the ships and escape pods leaving, no one noticed the *Millennium Falcon* flying toward the Star Destroyer's cargo bay.

The rebels were starting the final phase of their operation.

"I still say this plan is nuts," Han said as they ran to the main reactor engine room.

"We can do it," Leia insisted. "All we need to do is eject the reactor into space before it blows up."

If they made the jump to hyperspace in the Star Destroyer at the *exact* moment of the explosion, they could get away while convincing the Empire that the ship had been destroyed.

When they reached the engine room, Luke was waiting for them.

"Quick, Chewie," he said, "switch to auxiliary power and calculate the coordinates for the jump to hyperspace."

"*RRRRRWAAAHHHH!*" replied Chewie.

Then Luke and Leia worked furiously to disconnect the reactor from the ship. "I can't override the controls," Leia exclaimed. "It's not releasing the reactor."

Luke took a deep breath. He felt the Force flow through him. "We can do this," he said. "We have to!"

Luke trusted in the Force and let it guide his movements. His fingers flew over the control panel.

"There!" he cried. He had successfully released the reactor. He pressed the eject button. "Chewie, make the jump, now! Before—"

KA-BOOM!

The reactor shot into space and exploded in a massive fireball.

At that exact moment, Chewie jumped the Star Destroyer into hyperspace.

The admiral and his crew watched in shock from their escape pods. They couldn't believe it. Their Star Destroyer had been blown to pieces. . . .

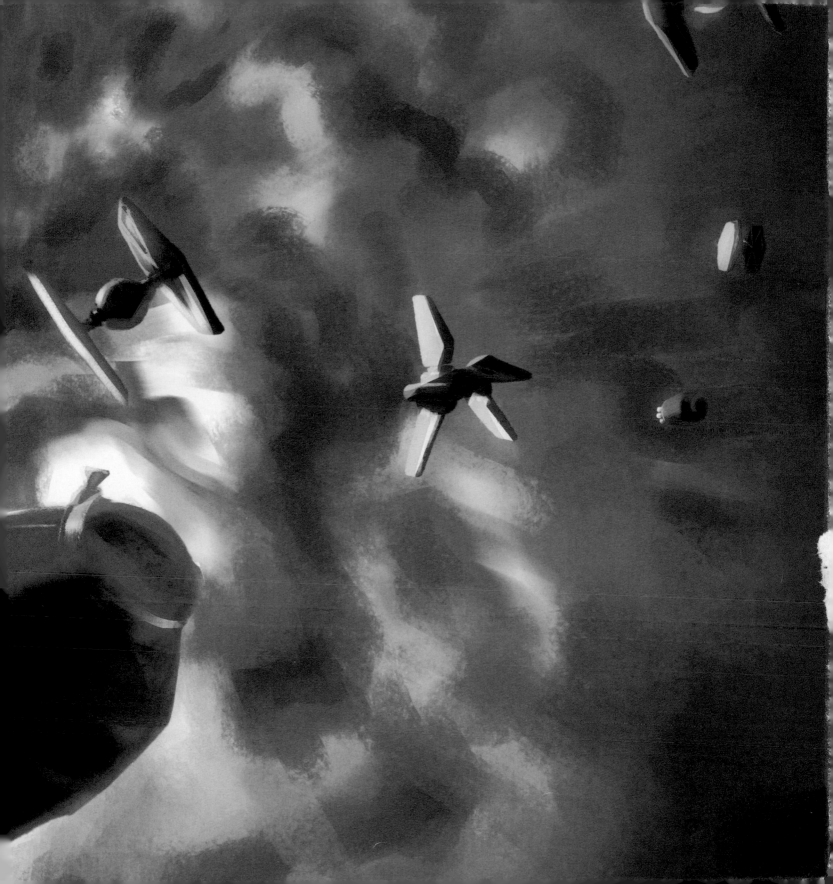

Except that it hadn't.

"We did it!" Luke, Leia, and Han cheered. Chewie roared with relief. They had escaped light-years away, and the Rebellion had its very own Star Destroyer.

"I wouldn't have believed it unless I'd seen it with my own eyes," said Han.

"And you said our plan was crazy," Leia teased.

"Because it was!" Han insisted.

Luke smiled.

"You're right," he said. "Just crazy enough to actually work."

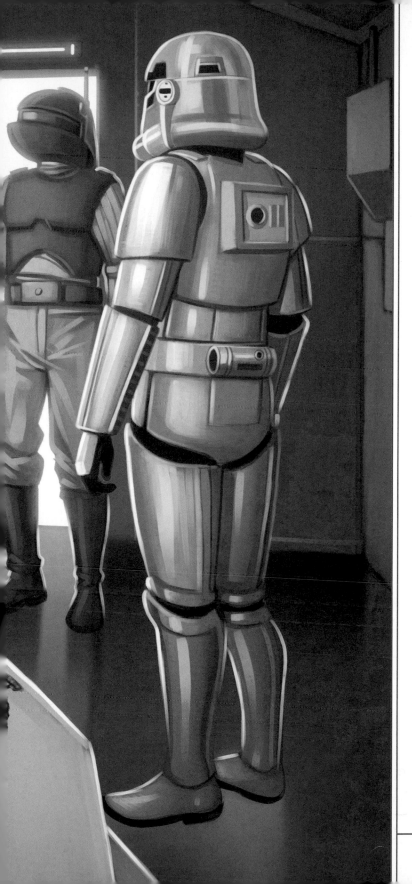

C-3PO WAS IN DANGER!

Stormtroopers had captured him and were holding him prisoner aboard a Star Destroyer. They planned to make C-3PO tell them where his friends Luke Skywalker, Han Solo, Princess Leia, and the rebel fleet were hiding.

The only thing was . . . C-3PO didn't know.

The stormtroopers contacted Darth Vader. "The droid is useless. He doesn't know where the secret rebel base is. We will scrap him for parts."

"I beg your pardon!" C-3PO exclaimed. "I am quite an important figure to the Rebel Alliance. My friends simply will not rest until I am safe."

C-3PO hoped help was on the way . . . and fast!

Help *was* on the way. But not from whom C-3PO expected.

R2-D2 had stolen an X-wing and charted a course to the Star Destroyer where C-3PO was being held captive.

Once there, he shut down all the power to make it look like his ship was drifting in space.

"Our scans show no signs of life," the Star Destroyer's Imperial crew members told their captain.

"Bring it on board," the captain ordered. "It might have information about the rebel fleet's hiding place."

R2-D2's trick had worked!

As soon as R2-D2's ship was docked in the cargo bay, stormtroopers surrounded it.
How was one little droid going to get past so many guards?
The stormtroopers contacted their captain.
"Looks like there's nothing on board the ship except a droid. What should we do?"
"Take it apart and scan its memory banks," the captain ordered from the
control room.
Now R2-D2 was really in trouble.

ZAP!

Quick as a flash, R2-D2 stunned the stormtrooper examining him.

"What the—?" exclaimed the others. "The droid is attacking! Blast it!"

The stormtroopers drew their blasters, but before they could fire a single shot, R2-D2 stunned *all* of them!

"*Beedo-deedo-thwarrrk!*" R2-D2 rolled away.

He was on a mission to save his friend, and nothing was going to stop him.

"We've lost contact with the stormtrooper team," the crew members in the control room told their captain. "The last thing they reported was something about a droid."

"Are you saying a *droid* took down an entire team of stormtroopers?" the captain asked angrily. "Send down more troops. Tell them to be on the lookout for the biggest, *nastiest* droid they've ever seen!"

Thankfully, R2-D2 did not look big *or* nasty. R2-D2 looked small and harmless, so he was able to roll past many stormtroopers without raising suspicion.

But while R2-D2 was small, he was far from harmless.

As he searched for his friend, he locked one team of stormtoopers in a cargo bay, confined a second set of soldiers behind a blast door, and then trapped a third team of troopers in a trash compactor.

"How did we even *get* down here?" one of the stormtroopers said. It had all happened so fast.

But R2-D2 was running out of time. More stormtroopers would be on the way soon, and he had to find C-3PO before his friend was scrapped for parts!

He searched every containment cell until, finally . . .

"It's about time!" C-3PO cried when R2-D2 opened the door to his cell. Two Imperial droids hovered over him, about to dismantle him.

"What took you so long?" C-3PO asked.

But R2-D2 didn't reply. He just rolled to the side.

"Where do you think you're going?" C-3PO exclaimed as he struggled against his restraints. "You're supposed to save me!"

WHIZ! ZAP! FIZZZZZ!

The stormtroopers chasing R2-D2 entered the cell and opened fire . . . but they hit the interrogation droids by mistake.

R2-D2 and C-3PO were able to sneak away in all the confusion.

The droids raced to the cargo bay. They had to escape in the X-wing before the captain realized what had happened.

"Where are the rest of the rebels?" C-3PO asked.

"*Beep-beebo-whirp*," R2-D2 replied.

"What do you mean it's just *you*?" C-3PO exclaimed. "Artoo-Detoo, you silly bucket of bolts, whatever were you thinking? Oh, I'm going to have to save our circuits myself, aren't I?"

As C-3PO talked, R2-D2 helped his friend aboard the X-wing and swiftly piloted their ship into space.

Meanwhile, the captain of the Star Destroyer was *not* happy.

"Whoever that intruder is, he's just taken out three dozen troops!"

"Sir, he's escaping in the X-wing," a crewman reported. "We're activating the tractor beam before they can jump to hyperspace."

"Never mind that!" the captain yelled. "Blast that ship before Darth Vader hears!"

Unfortunately, Darth Vader had already heard.

"I will deal with you later," he told the captain. "For now, I will follow that escaped rebel ship . . . myself!"

Darth Vader chased after the escaped X-wing in his TIE fighter.

R2-D2 zigged and zagged, but he was no match for the evil Sith Lord.

"That droid pilot has learned well . . . from someone," Darth Vader mused. He locked on his torpedoes. "But not well enough."

It looked as though it was all over for the two droids, until . . .

ZZZZZZAP!

A blast rocked Darth Vader's TIE fighter!

It was Princess Leia and Han Solo in the *Millennium Falcon* and Luke Skywalker in his X-wing. They had come to the rescue!

"Shooting at Vader never gets old," said Han.

Luke contacted the droids in their X-wing.

"Artoo, lock on to these coordinates and make the jump to hyperspace. Now!"

In a burst of light, the rebel ships escaped. They were all safe, and C-3PO had been rescued.

"Thank heavens you came in time," C-3PO said to R2-D2 once they were back with the fleet. "Though, it was my calm under pressure that really saved us all."

"*Budda-budda-thwark!*" R2-D2 replied.

"See, you go and say things like that, and it makes me wonder why I'm so nice to you," C-3PO said. "The stormtroopers were nicer to me than you."

The two droids continued to bicker, but deep down, they were happy to be back together again.

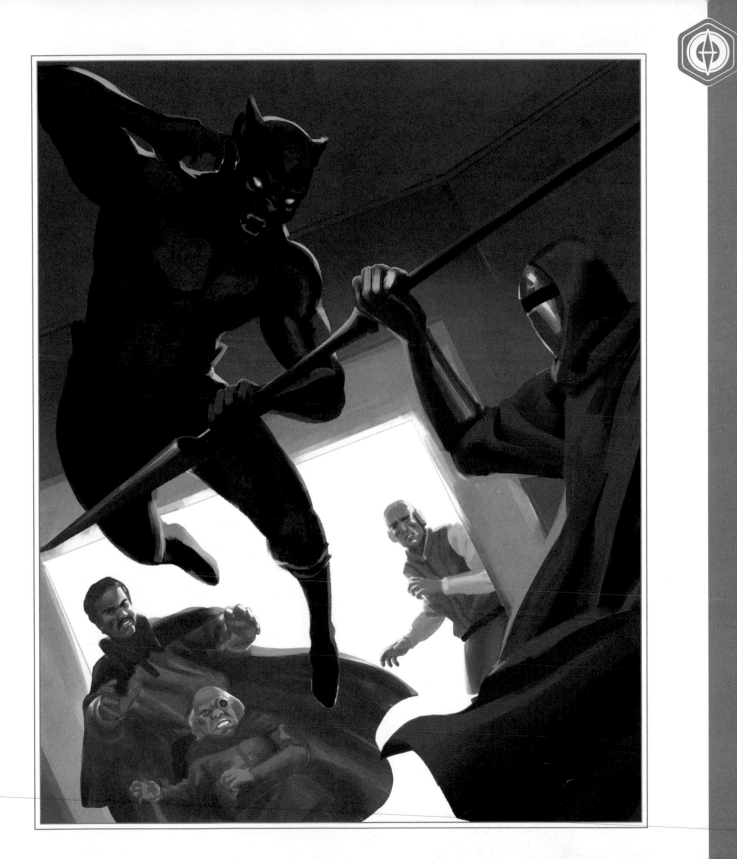

LANDO CALRISSIAN WAS A RISK TAKER,

and as everyone knows, risks are . . . well . . . risky. Sometimes things work out and the risk pays off. But then again, sometimes—perhaps even *most* times— things don't work out and the risk taker has to deal with the consequences.

Lando Calrissian *always* believed a risk would pay off, though.

"If we take this job for Toren, we could wipe out all our debt!" Lando said excitedly.

Toren was *Papa* Toren, a notorious crime lord. The job was to steal a spaceship.

Simple, right?

Lando's partner, Lobot, wasn't so sure.

Lando knew if they were going to pull off the heist, they would need help. More important, they would need to have *muscle*—warriors—on hand, just in case things became . . . challenging.

So Lando took Lobot to recruit two of the best fighters he had ever known: the ferocious and catlike Aleksin and Pavol. Lando didn't know if they were brothers or clones, but he didn't care. All he knew was that they were good at what they did and they were willing to join his crew.

Lobot couldn't believe Lando's luck.

There was one more person Lando needed to pull off the new mission—an old friend named Korin who was a former professor at an important university.

Well, *friend* probably wasn't the right word.

"There's nothing you can say that would make me work with a gurting bask like you ever again!" said Korin, pointing a blaster at Lando and Lobot.

But then Lando explained the job.

They weren't stealing any old ship. Papa Toren had heard that this specific ship belonged to an art collector. It was sure to be full of rare and, Lando hoped, priceless artifacts. Lando needed Korin to help identify the loot, and fortunately, Korin loved relics.

With his team assembled, Lando was ready to execute their plan. The first stop was the Sienar Fleet Systems Orbital Shipyard CC-24, where the ship was docked. It was a place that repaired starships.

It was also operated by the Empire.

Using special stealth spacesuits, the team drifted down to the shipyard.

"Getting in will be easy!" Lando had said.

Lobot had rolled his eyes. Whenever Lando said something was going to be *easy*, that meant it was going to be extremely hard.

But apart from a few stormtroopers, whom Aleksin and Pavol quickly took care of, the team was actually able to sneak on board the starship unnoticed. Once again, Lobot couldn't believe Lando's luck.

Before anyone at the shipyard even knew what was happening, Lando had fired up the ship and they were zooming off into open space.

"Woo-hoo!" shouted Lando. "Easy money! Easy money!"

"I'll believe it when I see it," said Lobot.

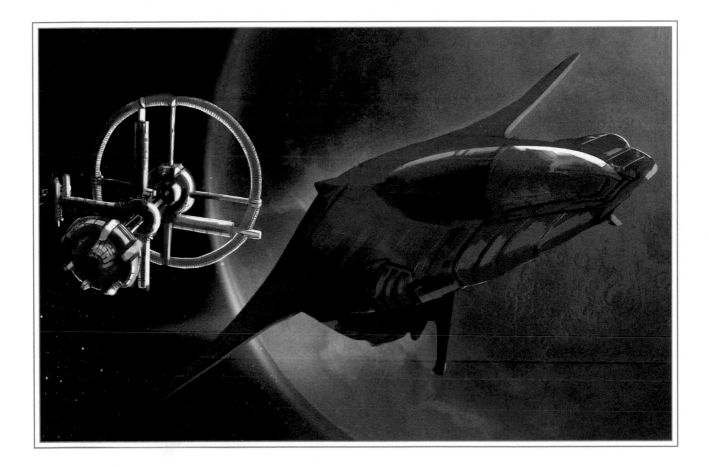

Lobot just wanted to get as far away from the shipyard as possible.

But then he saw what was waiting for them out in space. . . .

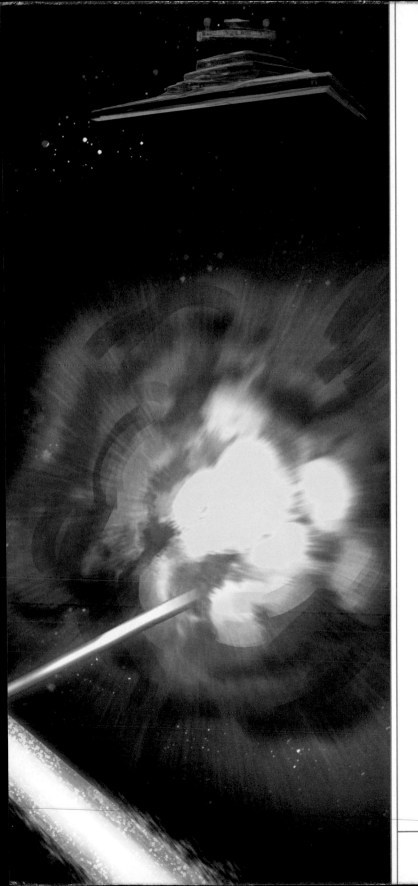

Three enormous Star Destroyers loomed in front of the newly stolen ship!

Lando realized that the ship must be even more valuable than he had thought.

Suddenly, one of the Destroyers opened fire.

ZZZRAK!

The blast didn't hit their ship, but it was close. The Empire clearly didn't want to *destroy* the ship; it just wanted to stop the ship from getting away. One of the Star Destroyers even deployed two gravity-based mines that would attach themselves to the stolen ship's hull to keep Lando and his team from making the leap to hyperspace.

But before Lando could even push a button, an automatic defense system on board the starship kicked in and destroyed the two mines!

Lando *really* liked that ship.

Two of the Star Destroyers activated their tractor beams, trying to grab on to the starship. But Lando was an incredible pilot. He flew the stolen ship so close to the Star Destroyers that the tractor beams missed the starship entirely and hit each other instead.

The two enormous ships crashed right into each other.

Then Lando punched the starship's hyperdrive, and they were out of there.

Lando had done it! With the help of his crew, he had stolen the ship from the Imperial shipyard and even outwitted three Star Destroyers.

Now all they had to do was take the starship back to Papa Toren, but first Lando wanted to see the loot they had so brilliantly made off with.

Korin led them all down one of the artifact-lined hallways to a blast door.

"This is the only area of the ship I haven't been able to access," Korin explained. "It's a central chamber and it is *very* well secured."

Lando was almost giddy at the thought of what could be inside, and he knew Lobot could hack any code that was keeping the door off limits.

Lobot agreed to help, but he'd had a bad feeling about the mission from the start, and he sensed that whatever was behind that door would only make things worse.

Lobot was right.

As soon as the blast door opened, two deadly red guards burst through!

Well, this definitely qualifies as "challenging," Lando thought as Aleksin and Pavol leapt into action.

Everyone in the galaxy knew that the red-robed Imperial Royal Guard was an elite group of killers trained specifically to protect the Emperor. They were his personal bodyguards, handpicked from the very best of his forces.

But the two who were protecting the ship had clearly never encountered the likes of Aleksin and Pavol. It was by no means an easy fight, but the two ferocious warriors soon defeated the guards.

It looked like Lando's good luck was back on track.

That was, until Korin had to ruin everything.

"There's only one person who could possibly own this ship," Korin said.

Lando thought through their mission.

The glamorous starship. The three Star Destroyers. The rare treasures from across the galaxy on board. The red-robed killers.

It all made sense.

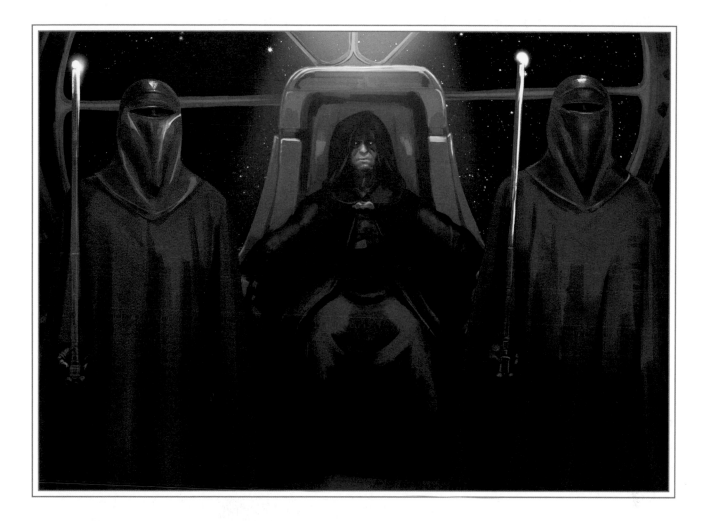

Across the galaxy, Emperor Palpatine, the evil Sith Lord and the supreme leader of the Empire, learned that his priceless ship, full of some of his greatest treasures, had been stolen.

No smuggler could do such a thing and live to tell the tale.

The Emperor would use the full force of his Imperial Navy to hunt down his missing ship and make sure of that fact.

"So the ship belongs to the *Emperor*," Lando replied with a nervous chuckle. "We can get out of this one. We'll just sneak away in an escape pod. It will be easy!"

But Lobot wasn't so sure.

It seemed as though Lando's luck had finally run out. . . .

PRINCESS LEIA ORGANA WAS ON A SECRET MISSION.

She was leading Imperial ships on a great space chase across the galaxy.

Leia needed to distract the Empire so the Rebel Alliance could prepare for war.

The next stop on her mission was the volcanic planet of Sesid.

Ace pilot Nien Nunb, veteran commando Lokmarcha, communications specialist Kidi, and demolitions expert Antrot accompanied Leia.

Aboard Nien's ship, the *Mellcrawler*, the team touched down on a giant lily pad. Leia planned to meet a mysterious freedom fighter known as Captain Aurelant on Sesid. They hoped Aurelant could help them distract the Empire and would perhaps even join the Rebellion.

In town, Leia and her friends tried to blend in with the island tourists, but there was no time for fun. They had work to do!

While Nien stayed with the ship, Leia and the rest of the team boarded a boat. They skimmed across the waves toward a nearby island, where they would meet Aurelant and send out a beacon to attract the Empire.

When they reached the island, Lokmarcha led Kidi and Antrot to the top of a volcano to activate the beacon while Leia waited for Aurelant on the black-sand beach below.

Hours passed with no sign of Aurelant. The team decided to return to the *Mellcrawler*. Antrot was relieved; he had been worried that the volcano would erupt. Lokmarcha explained that there were tall, black escape pods all over the island in case of emergency.

But as Leia looked out across the water, it became clear that an active volcano was the least of their worries. . . .

The beacon had worked! Stormtroopers were streaking along the surface of the ocean on waveskimmers and firing at the team of rebels.

Leia opened the throttle, sending their boat across the waves, while Lokmarcha fired at the Imperials.

As Leia veered their boat side to side to avoid enemy fire, Kidi alerted Nien to take off and await further instructions. Leia told Antrot to arm detonators and throw them into the water to slow down the troopers.

But Antrot's detonators were no match for the Imperials, and the rebels were soon surrounded.

It was only a matter of time before their boat had been blasted.

Smoke began to pour from their damaged vessel as the waveskimmers drew closer. Leia scanned the horizon, hoping to find an island they could reach before their boat sank into the ocean.

Suddenly, a massive shadow appeared in the water beneath them! When the shadow broke the surface, Leia saw that it was a submarine vehicle dripping with shaggy seaweed.

The strange vessel opened like a huge mouth and swallowed the team's boat whole before sinking back beneath the waves. The rebels couldn't tell if they were being rescued or captured.

Inside, aliens with red eyes and sharp teeth surrounded the team, brandishing blasters and knives as they took away the rebels' weapons. They were Draedan pirates, and they easily outnumbered Leia and her crew.

Then a massive tattooed Draedan pushed through the crowd and stood right in front of Leia. The princess held her ground, but the other rebels were sure they had been defeated . . .

. . . until the leader introduced himself as Captain Aurelant!

The team was relieved. They had been rescued.

Leia contacted Nien, who was equally glad to hear that his team was all right. But he informed Leia that they needed to get off the island immediately. An Imperial Star Destroyer was lurking above Sesid, and there were more on the way.

Leia had no idea how they would rendezvous with Nien and the *Mellcrawler*, but Aurelant had a plan.

It turned out the escape pods on the volcanic island *would* come in handy.

As the team boarded one of the pods, Aurelant promised to have his friends release escape pods all over Sesid so the Empire wouldn't be able to tell which one held the rebels.

Leia thanked Aurelant for his help, and moments later their pod rocketed away!

All across Sesid, escape pods shot into the sky. Puzzled stormtroopers and Imperial officers watched as hundreds of pods rocketed toward space, leaving bright streaks behind them.

Nien homed in on Leia's comlink and retrieved the team.

Back on board the *Mellcrawler*, the rebels celebrated another successful mission. But their job was far from over.

If there was any hope of defeating the Empire, Leia needed to keep the Imperials distracted by remaining a moving target.

The great space chase would continue!

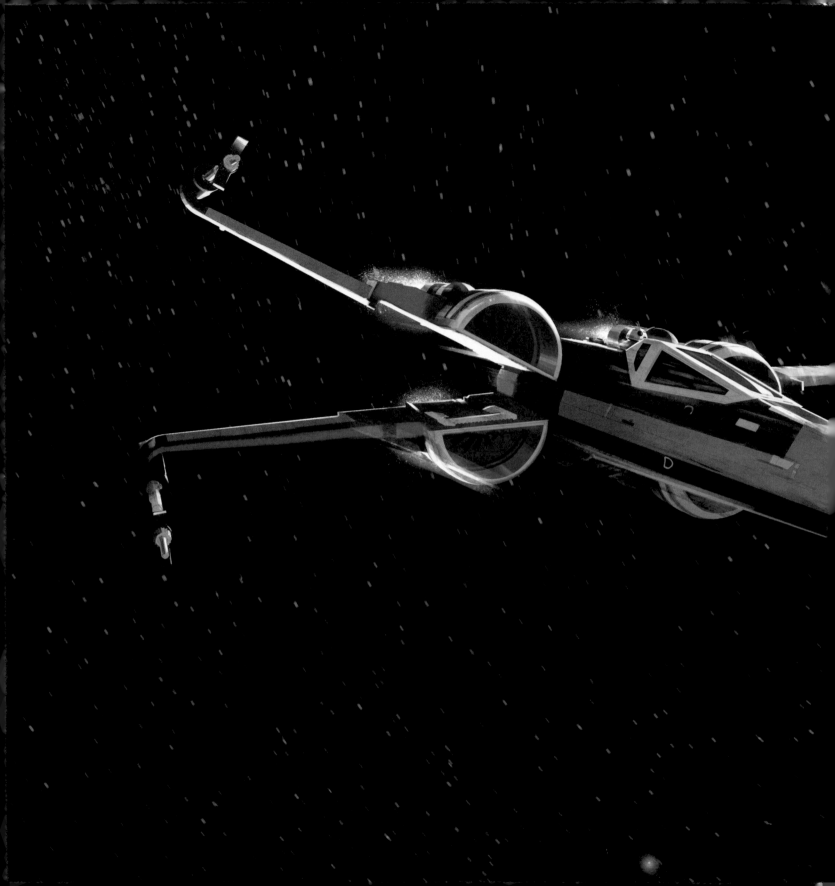

POE DAMERON ROCKETED THROUGH SPACE IN HIS X-WING FIGHTER.

Poe was a commander for the New Republic's navy, and he spent his days patrolling the Outer Rim with a small team of pilots and his faithful droid, BB-8.

But this was no ordinary day.

Something unusual had popped up on Poe's scanner. It was a distress signal from a ship called the *Yissira Zyde*.

BB-8 sent the information to Poe's fellow pilots, and the three X-wings jumped to lightspeed. They needed to reach the *Yissira Zyde*, and fast!

When Poe's squadron came out of lightspeed, they were shocked to see a fleet of First Order TIE fighters buzzing around the helpless ship.

The First Order was an evil shadow of the Galactic Empire that was slowly rising to power. But it seemed to be more dangerous than anyone realized.

Some of the TIE fighters streaked toward Poe's squadron and opened fire, but Poe and his fellow pilots were ready for them.

The three X-wings dipped and weaved among the First Order ships, expertly avoiding enemy fire and taking down TIE after TIE.

But before Poe's team could reach the *Yissira Zyde*, a glow began to rise from its stern. In the blink of an eye, the freighter and the First Order ships had stretched and snapped into hyperspace!

When the squadron returned to its base, Poe urged his superiors to do something to help the *Yissira Zyde*. But everyone he spoke with ordered him not to interfere. They didn't believe that the First Order was as dangerous as Poe claimed.

Poe knew he would get in trouble if he disobeyed orders. But he also knew that the crew of the *Yissira Zyde* was in real danger. He needed to help them—especially if no one else was going to.

BB-8 homed in on where the First Order had taken the missing ship, and Poe's X-wing made the jump to lightspeed. The little droid also discovered that the stolen ship had been carrying powerful weapons at the time of the attack.

Poe wasn't surprised that the First Order wanted the weapons, but he needed to find out where it was taking them.

BB-8 shrieked when they came out of lightspeed. Before them floated almost the entire First Order fleet: Star Destroyers, frigates, cruisers, and TIE fighters! But the *Yissira Zyde* was nowhere in sight.

The one thing Poe and BB-8 had going for them was the element of surprise: not the surprise of an X-wing's appearance in the middle of a First Order fleet but, rather, the surprise of what they did next.

Poe and BB-8 charged!

Poe pushed his X-wing fighter to its limits. He banked right and looped left while blasting at every First Order ship that stood in his way.

Meanwhile, BB-8 continued to search for a signal from the missing ship, but the First Order was closing in!

Poe flew so close to one of the First order frigates that he could actually see stormtroopers staring at him through the windows as he raced past. The TIE fighters stopped shooting at him, because they didn't want to hit one of their own ships!

Suddenly, BB-8 beeped wildly! He had located the *Yissira Zyde's* tracking signal! The ship was inside one of the Star Destroyers. Poe had to tell his superiors as soon as possible.

As more TIEs closed in, Poe punched the controls and they rocketed to lightspeed, leaving the First Order behind!

Poe returned to the base, happy that he had discovered the location of the missing ship. But a military officer and two guards were waiting for him. Poe knew he was in trouble.

The officer introduced himself as Major Ematt and ushered Poe and BB-8 to a waiting speeder. They traveled to a different part of the base, where Ematt led Poe to a stand-alone bunker.

Poe entered alone and immediately recognized the woman sitting at a desk in front of him. It was General Leia Organa!

Leia had once been a princess and had helped her brother—Jedi Knight Luke Skywalker—destroy the evil Empire. But the First Order had risen from the ashes of the Empire, and now Leia needed Poe's help.

Leia asked Poe to tell her all about the First Order and the missing ship. The general listened very carefully as Poe recounted his entire adventure. When he was finished, Leia promised to do everything she could to help rescue the *Yissira Zyde*. Then she asked Poe if he had ever heard of the Resistance.

That was the day everything changed for Poe Dameron.

Poe and his squadron agreed to join General Organa and become part of the Resistance against the First Order.

Poe had been a pilot, but now he would have a chance to be a hero.

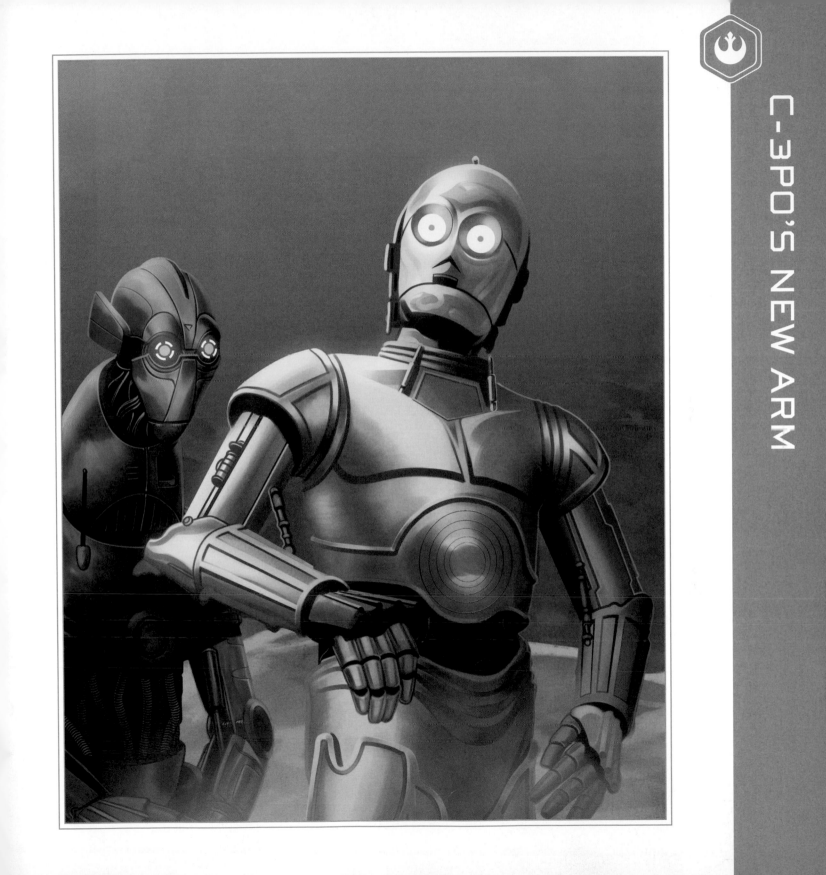

"I MUST SAY,"

C-3PO exclaimed to BB-8 and Poe Dameron, "I don't know what I would have done if you hadn't come to rescue me."

The droid had just returned from a top-secret mission for the Resistance.

"Let's just get you to maintenance," Poe Dameron said. "We have to get you all fixed up."

BB-8 whistled in agreement and rolled down the corridor, leading the way. "Oh, yes, Master Dameron. I had almost forgotten!" C-3PO looked down. He was missing an arm!

"What happened back there, buddy?" Poe asked as he led the way through the base.

"Well, Master Dameron, it all started when our ship was attacked," C-3PO said. As they made their way to maintenance, C-3PO told Poe and BB-8 all about his adventure. . . .

C-3PO had been separated from his friends when his ship crash-landed on a strange planet. All he had for company were five other droids. There was PZ-99, a military droid; C-O34, a construction droid; 2M2, a medical droid; and VL-44, a security droid.

Most important, there was Omri. He was the reason for the top-secret mission. Omri worked for the First Order and had important information about the location of Admiral Ackbar, a Resistance leader who had been captured.

C-3PO didn't trust Omri one bit.

The droids had picked up a transmitter signal from a downed First Order ship a ways away. If they could get to the transmitter, C-3PO could contact the Resistance and they would be saved.

"We must work as a team if we are to leave this dreadful place," C-3PO told Omri. "And as such, I feel we should put our differences aside."

"I agree . . ." Omri said. "For now."

He didn't trust C-3PO, either.

With that, the six droids began the long journey to the transmitter.

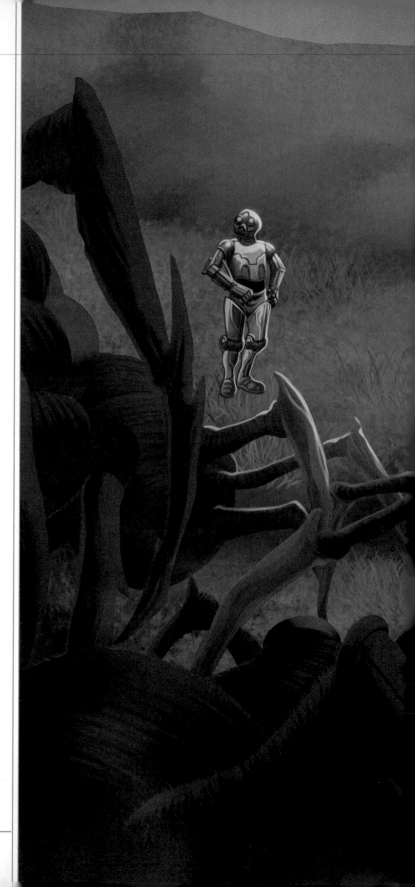

They hadn't walked far when the ground around the droids erupted.

There were space spiders everywhere!

"Quickly, everyone!" C-3PO called, narrowly avoiding a space spider's pincers. The droids had to escape before they were overrun.

PZ-99 ran in front of the group to protect the other droids. The military droid attacked the space spiders, giving his companions just enough time to escape.

Soon the droids had left the space spiders and PZ-99 far behind.

Omri was confused. Why had PZ-99 stayed behind?

C-3PO explained that PZ-99 had wanted to protect his friends. But Omri still didn't understand. A droid in the First Order would never have done what PZ-99 had done.

The droids didn't have much time to rest after the spider attack, because a huge lake of oil blocked their path. C-O34, the construction droid, had a solution. He could form a bridge! The droids started to cross C-O34 when—*SPLASH!*—a huge aquatic beast jumped out of the oil.

VL-44 beeped in alarm as the droids were attacked by the oil monster's tentacles.

"Yes, VeeEl. We're moving as fast as we can!" C-3PO cried.

Then a tentacle wrapped itself around Threepio and started to pull him under!

"I've got you!" said Omri, the First Order droid, pulling C-3PO free. But C-3PO's arm had been lost to the beast.

C-3PO was surprised. Losing an arm was shocking, but he hadn't expected the First Order droid to rescue him, either.

The droids were able to cross the oil thanks to the bridge C-O34 formed, but the construction droid had taken too much damage during the fight and couldn't continue on the journey.

C-3PO didn't think he could continue the journey, either, but they had to get Omri's information back to the Resistance. The droids had battled all kinds of creatures. What else could remain?

C-3PO wished he hadn't asked himself that question as they were suddenly attacked by a swarm of huge insectoids!

"Quickly! Keep moving!" Omri urged C-3PO.

In all the chaos, C-3PO and Omri were separated from VL-44 and 2M2.

C-3PO and Omri had only each other at that point—a Resistance droid and a First Order droid. As they continued their journey, walking across a vast and lonely desert for a very, very long time, C-3PO wondered how their adventure could possibly end.

When it began to rain, C-3PO worried about rust, but he soon realized they were in far more danger than he had thought.

Acid rain was falling from the sky!

"We are as good as destroyed if we don't get to shelter!" C-3PO cried.

The droids ran under a piece of the crashed ship, just in sight of the transmitter. They had been so close to calling for help.

Omri then looked at C-3PO and made a decision.

"You have a mission," Omri said. "There is nothing in my directive telling me to prevent you from completing it."

Omri then shared the location where the First Order was holding Admiral Ackbar so C-3PO could inform the Resistance.

"I don't understand," C-3PO replied. "You are changing sides?"

"I am not choosing sides," Omri said. "I'm choosing friendship."

And with that, the First Order droid bravely ran into the acid rain to activate the transmitter.

Back at the base, C-3PO finished his story. "You found me thanks to Omri."

C-3PO left Poe and BB-8 and went down to maintenance, where the droids there could attach Omri's red arm to the golden protocol droid. It had been all that was left of the First Order droid when Poe and BB-8 came to rescue C-3PO.

"Good as new," C-3PO said to himself. He had decided to wear the red arm with pride to help him remember their surprising friendship. C-3PO would never forget what Omri had done for him, and the Resistance.

REY WAS A SCAVENGER.

Rey had lived alone on the desert planet of Jakku since she was a little girl, waiting for her family to come back and find her.

She spent each day searching wrecked ships from long ago battles for parts she could trade with the alien Unkar Plutt for food.

It was time-consuming, hard work, and sometimes it was very dangerous. Rey had to fight off other scavengers—like Teedos—to protect her finds, and sometimes there were giant sand storms that lasted for days. But it was the only life Rey had ever known.

One day, after a very long sand storm, Rey left home to begin another day of work. The storm had covered many of her favorite wrecks, and the newly revealed wrecks had already been claimed by the Teedos or other scavengers. If she didn't find something soon, she wouldn't have anything to trade with Unkar for food that day.

But then, far off in the distance, Rey saw something glisten on the horizon.

Rey could hardly believe it. It was a ship—and not a wreck like the ones she had picked over her entire life. It was a real intact ship!

The ship wasn't ready to fly. It needed to be fixed up a little, but Rey knew that if she could get it flying again, she could trade it with Unkar for more portions than she had ever seen before. She would no longer be hungry all the time, and she wouldn't have to work so hard every day.

Rey threw herself into fixing the ship. She worked tirelessly, spending each day scavenging for pieces she needed for the ship or for parts she could trade with Unkar for supplies for the ship.

Her stomach constantly grumbled, but she kept telling herself that the portions she would get for the ship once it was ready would make the long hunger-filled days worthwhile.

Many days into her secret project, Rey was in town washing off a new piece she had found for the ship.

"What're you building?" someone asked.

Rey looked up in alarm. It was another scavenger, Devi. So far, no one had discovered the ship Rey was working on. She had been so careful. Had someone learned her secret?

"I'm not building anything," Rey said.

But Devi didn't look like she believed Rey. Devi and her partner, Strunk, told Rey they had noticed she didn't trade all the parts she found. They knew she was hiding something.

Rey shrugged them off, leaving Niima Outpost as quickly as she could, but she knew that wouldn't be the last she'd see of Devi and Strunk.

A few days later, Rey was working on her ship when she heard someone calling her name.

It was Devi. She and Strunk had followed Rey to the ship.

"What do you want?" Rey asked.

"We can help you fix this thing up, Rey," Devi said. All they wanted in return was for Rey to take them with her when she used the ship to fly away from Jakku.

But Rey planned to sell the ship, not fly away in it. She couldn't leave Jakku. She was still waiting for her family.

Devi and Strunk didn't understand why Rey wouldn't want to leave Jakku, but they agreed to take some of the portions Unkar would give Rey for the ship instead.

"What do you say," Devi asked. "Partners?"

With Devi and Strunk's help, the repairs to the ship went very quickly.

Soon the ship was finished and all they had to do was try flying it to make sure it actually worked.

Years before, Rey had found pieces of a flight simulator scattered across the dunes. Instead of selling them to Unkar, she had put them back together so she could spend her evenings practicing flying across the stars. She was pretty good at the simulations, but flying this ship would be real!

The three scavengers gathered in the ship's cockpit. Rey nervously gripped the controls.

With a great *VROOM* the ship started. Devi and Strunk looked terrified, and for a moment so was Rey. But then the ship lurched into the sky, and she suddenly felt weightless—and free.

Rey flew the ship across the surface of the planet, smiling as it responded to her movement of the controls. It banked and swerved and circled just as she told it to. It was perfect.

That night, Rey couldn't sleep at all. She kept thinking about how free she felt soaring above the dunes.

Even though it was the middle of the night, Rey decided to go back to check on the ship, just to make sure it hadn't all been a dream.

The ship was still there, but it wasn't alone. Four shadowy figures lurked nearby. They were Teedos!

Rey grabbed her staff and ran out to stand right in front of the ship.

"This is mine!" Rey shouted. "It's my ship, do you understand? You can't have it."

Suddenly, a shot rang out. But it wasn't from one of the Teedos.

"You heard her!" yelled Devi. "It's *her* ship!"

Devi and Strunk helped Rey chase the Teedos away.

Rey was thankful for their help. Why had it taken her so long to trust her fellow scavengers?

Rey, Devi, and Strunk agreed that it was time to sell the ship to Unkar, before anyone else tried to steal it.

The next day, Rey once again took her place in the cockpit and flew the ship to Niima Outpost. It felt so good to fly. It almost made her want to keep the ship and fly off into the stars.

Almost. But not quite. Her stomach rumbled. She needed the portions. And she couldn't risk missing her family if they returned for her.

Rey set the ship down and turned to her companions.

"Don't let anyone else on board," she said. "Only me and Unkar."

Unkar was waiting for Rey in the shipyard, amazed. He had never expected Rey would bring him such a treasure.

Rey was proud of the ship. She couldn't stop smiling.

But then Rey heard a familiar VROOM.
Sand swirled up and a hot blast of air hit her.
The smile fell from Rey's face.
Devi and Strunk had stolen the ship and left Jakku.

Her ship was gone.

The portions she had been dreaming about all that time were gone.

And something else was gone, too: the feeling of freedom she had known when she was flying the ship—a *real* ship, not a simulator.

The next day, Rey got up early. Nothing had really changed. She still needed to scavenge for parts to trade with Unkar. But then again, something *inside* Rey had changed. She was determined to fly again. There was always hope.

After all, if she had found a ship, who knew what else she might find out on the dunes. . . .

BEFORE HE WAS KNOWN AS FINN . . . BEFORE HE ESCAPED

from the First Order . . .
before he joined the Resistance . . .

FN-2187 was a member of a four-person stormtrooper team.

One day, FN-2187's team was battling its way toward the heart of an enemy base. His team needed to destroy a bunker up ahead.

As always, FN-2187 led the charge, calling the shots. Behind him, FN-2199 and FN-2000 moved quickly. But the fourth member of their team, FN-2003, had fallen behind.

Everyone called him Slip, because that's what he always seemed to be doing—slipping up.

FN-2187 knew Slip wouldn't last long by himself. But how could his team go back and rescue Slip without failing the mission?

Thinking fast, FN-2187 told the other two members of his team to run ahead while he ran back to help Slip. Then without missing a beat, FN-2187 charged the enemy bunker, dodging blast after blast. He slid into the bunker and detonated his grenade.

FN-2187 and his team had finished their mission, together.

The world fell silent . . . and then everything flickered and disappeared.

FN-2187 blinked a few times, clearing his vision. It was always a little strange when a battle simulation ended and he found himself back in the simulation room. But that was his life as a stormtrooper: endless training in the simulation room, preparing for the day when he would see a *real* battle. And that day would come soon.

He just wasn't sure how he felt about it.

What FN-2187 didn't know was that he was being watched.

Captain Phasma and General Hux led the First Order stormtroopers, and they were concerned about FN-2187. They didn't understand why he had gone back to help Slip.

"A stormtrooper's loyalty must be to the First Order," said Captain Phasma. "Not to his comrades."

General Hux agreed. FN-2187 was a strong soldier, but he wasn't acting exactly the way a stormtrooper should.

They would have to keep a close eye on him.

Training continued. FN-2187 and his team worked hard. Every day they trained to be the best First Order soldiers they could be. And FN-2187 was the best of the best.

But he still didn't feel quite *right*. His heart just wasn't in it. Sometimes he wanted to ask his friends if they felt the same way.

But he could tell they didn't. He could tell they didn't have any doubts at all.

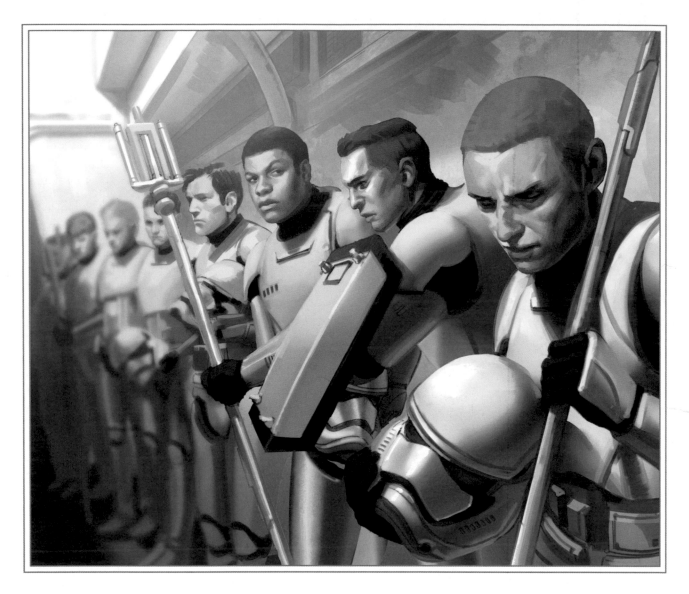

One day the stormtroopers were taken to an exercise room and handed different weapons. They were going to spend the day sparring with each other. Two stormtroopers would fight until one lost, and then the winner would fight the next trooper in line.

FN-2187 was excited about the new challenge, but he was concerned for his friend. Slip was up first.

Slip held his own for a while, dodging and stabbing with his force pike.
Whoosh! Zap!

FN-2187 was proud of his teammate. Slip was often the slowest and clumsiest of the team, but not that day. It was nice to see him doing well.

But then Slip . . . slipped. He faltered for a moment, and his opponent charged, knocking Slip to the ground.

FN-2187 watched with concern as his friend staggered back to the end of the line. Slip would have to fight again, and he wasn't looking so good.

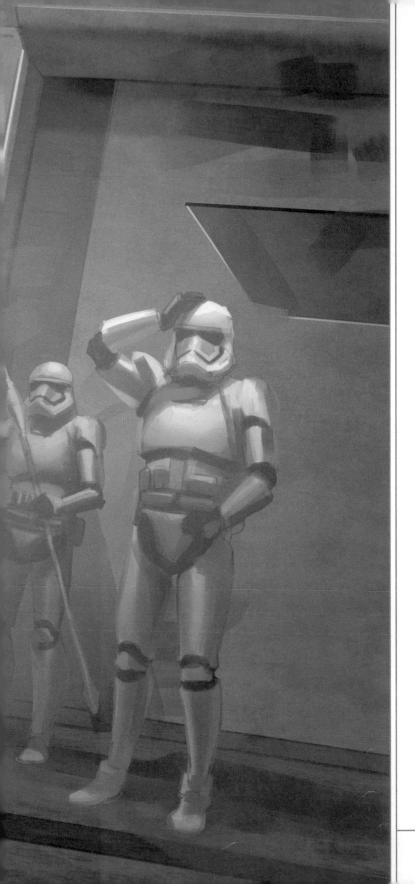

Soon it was FN-2187's turn. He was a strong fighter, and he beat three other stormtroopers before his teammate FN-2199 stepped up. Nines, as they all called him, came at FN-2187 hard and angry.

FN-2187 dodged back, surprised. His friend was fighting him as though he really wanted to hurt him.

Crash! Thwack!

And Nines really almost *did* hurt him before FN-2187 was finally able to take him down. FN-2187 was shaken, but he didn't have time to think about what had just happened, because the next person in line for him to fight . . .

. . . was Slip.

And Slip still didn't look so good.

FN-2187 almost wanted to let him win. It would be easy to throw the fight—to make it look as though he was so tired that even Slip could get a lucky blow in.

But then Slip would have to fight the next stormtrooper in the line. And that stormtrooper wouldn't care that Slip was injured. He wouldn't be careful with him the way FN-2187 would be.

So as gently and carefully as possible, FN-2187 defeated Slip.
Then he quickly helped his friend back to his feet.

FN-2187 was knocked out of the fighting in the next round. He couldn't stop thinking about what had happened.

When the day was over, Captain Phasma pulled him aside. She demanded an explanation.

"Eff-Enn-Two-Zero-Zero-Three had been injured," FN-2187 explained, using Slip's official stormtrooper designation. "I didn't want to see him hurt any further."

"You considered losing to him first, didn't you?" Phasma asked. "A real stormtrooper has no room for sympathy."

A real stormtrooper has no room for sympathy.

Phasma's words repeated in FN-2187's mind as he walked back to his bunk.

A real stormtrooper.

Maybe he wasn't a real stormtrooper after all.

FN-2187 wondered where that left him. Was there a place in the galaxy for a stormtrooper who wasn't a real stormtrooper?

FN-2187 could only hope that there was . . . and that he'd find it soon.

CAPTAIN PHASMA WAS IN TROUBLE.

Three Resistance fighters had somehow managed to get on the First Order's Starkiller Base: a planet that was also the greatest superweapon in the galaxy. They were a smuggler named Han Solo, a Wookiee named Chewbacca, and—most surprising—one of Phasma's former stormtroopers, FN-2187, who had left the First Order to help General Leia Organa's Resistance.

They had forced Phasma to lower the base's defense shields and then left her stranded in a garbage chute!

With the base's shields down, Resistance X-wings were able to make repeated attack runs from above. They were trying to destroy Starkiller Base!

First Order TIE fighters fought back against the starfighters, but Phasma knew the Resistance was going to win the battle, and it was all because of her.

Phasma didn't have much time to get out of the garbage chute and off the base before the planet was completely destroyed. Lucky for her, the Resistance's attacks had weakened the structure of the base enough so she could force her way out of the foul-smelling trap.

However, Phasma didn't just need to escape; she needed to erase any possible record of her betrayal. The First Order would never forgive her for helping the Resistance by lowering the defense shields, so she had to make sure no one ever found out.

But when Captain Phasma went to the nearest computer station to destroy all record of what she had done, she learned that someone else had already accessed the files: an officer named Sol Rivas.

Rivas had evidence that Phasma had helped the Resistance, so Phasma had no choice but to find him and stop him before he could share that information with General Hux of the First Order.

Phasma tracked Rivas outside, into the chaos of the battle between the First Order and the Resistance. He was headed for a repair hangar a short distance away, through the snow-covered forest. But the planet was starting to quake, and the very ground beneath Phasma's chromium boots began to tear apart.

In the distance, across a newly formed crevice that had ripped across the planet's surface, Phasma saw the glow of lightsabers clashing. It was the First Order's dark warrior Kylo Ren, battling a young but talented Resistance fighter named Rey.

But Phasma would not be distracted from her mission. She had to stop Rivas if she ever hoped to once again stand beside Kylo Ren and General Hux as a leader of the First Order.

By the time Captain Phasma reached the hangar, Rivas had already taken off in one of the two damaged TIE fighters held there. Phasma wasted no time boarding the second TIE and taking off after Rivas as Starkiller Base erupted in a shower of sparks behind her.

Captain Phasma followed Rivas to the nearby primitive planet of Luprora. Her examination of his abandoned TIE made it clear to Phasma that Rivas had landed there because he was out of fuel and that he had not been able to contact the First Order on his journey.

Phasma's secret was still safe—at least for now.

But she was wary of the eerie planet. It seemed abandoned, and while the tides were low at the moment, Phasma could tell that the rocky ground was covered by salt water most of the time.

She still needed to find Rivas, but she would have to be on high alert as she made her way around the edge of a nearby body of water in search of her enemy.

Suddenly, hideous sea creatures burst from the surface of the water! Phasma recognized them as r'ora, deadly tentacled beasts with razor-sharp teeth and claws.

Captain Phasma had to use every ounce of her training, experience, and strength to battle her way through the r'ora, and she relied heavily on her customized blaster rifle.

After battling the r'ora, the only way for Phasma to go was up.

With a large cliff face looming before her, she knew she had a long climb ahead.

But above was the only place where Rivas could be hiding.

Captain Phasma was a skilled climber, but her muscles burned after the battle with the r'ora. Steadily, she made her way up the wall of rock until she could finally pull herself up to a landing.

Sure enough, there was Rivas.

He was grateful to be rescued until he realized that Captain Phasma *wasn't* rescuing him.

Phasma knew he had the evidence that she had betrayed the First Order. Rivas pleaded with her, promising Phasma that he would never tell the First Order—or anyone else—that she had helped the Resistance,

But no amount of begging would do.

Captain Phasma had escaped from Starkiller Base. She had defeated the r'ora. And she had silenced Rivas.

Phasma had regained her power, but she still needed to reinforce her place within the First Order.

When she rejoined the fleet in space, Phasma reported to General Hux that *Rivas* was the traitor who had helped the Resistance destroy Starkiller Base, but that she had made sure he would never trouble them again.

"I should have known that nothing could impede your devotion to the First Order," said Hux.

And Phasma vowed to herself that, indeed, nothing ever would again.

ROSE TICO NEVER EXPECTED TO WORK FOR THE RESISTANCE.

She had grown up with her sister, Paige, in a peaceful corner of the galaxy, but then the First Order had arrived, bringing fear and destruction.

Rose and Paige had fled to General Leia Organa and the Resistance, who had welcomed them with open arms.

Now the two sisters fought for others who were trying to break free from the First Order's cruelty—like the people of Atterra Bravo. The First Order had blockaded the planet so nobody could come or go—not even to bring food. The Atterrans were starving and needed the Resistance's help.

General Organa had sent Rose, Paige, and a squadron of Resistance bombers to complete a series of four supply runs for the people of Atterra Bravo. But if the First Order realized what they were doing, there would be a battle . . . a battle that the small band of Resistance ships might not win.

Rose held her breath as they sped closer to the planet.

It helped to have Paige by her side. Rose and Paige always flew together. Paige's presence gave Rose a sense of peace, no matter how dangerous the mission.

But on that day, it seemed as though there was no need to worry.

The First Order was nowhere in sight.

Rose and Paige's bomber—the *Hammer*—finally reached the coordinates for their drop. They had made it!

Rose smiled as she watched the payload fall from their ship to the planet below. Soon the people of Atterra Bravo would have some of the food and supplies they desperately needed.

One after another, the rest of the Resistance ships dropped the first wave of supplies.

With one supply run finished, they just had three more to go. So the squadron turned to head back to their base on the ice planet of Refnu to reload for the next run.

Suddenly, a squadron of TIE fighters appeared and opened fire!
The Resistance ships were old and slow, but they were flown by talented pilots
and sharp-eyed gunners like Paige who fought back against the TIEs.

The blackness of space was lit with bright red and green blaster fire.
The TIE fighters swerved and veered, but one by one the enemy ships were destroyed—all except for a lone TIE that zoomed away from the battle.

"He's going to make a report for sure," Rose told Paige as they worked to reload the ships back at their base.

The TIE fighter pilot who had gotten away would have plenty to tell his commanders. The First Order would soon know that the Resistance was up to something, and running three more supply runs under its nose was beyond risky.

But Rose knew that the people of Atterra Bravo needed them. Even if her squadron's mission had just become far more dangerous, they couldn't give up.

They would just have to hope that nothing went wrong.

Of course, *everything* went wrong on the second run.

Squadrons of TIE fighters descended on the Resistance ships before they could deliver more supplies to the surface below.

Several of the bombers were destroyed.

But Rose and Paige worked together to devise a plan.

They decided to send the ships in two by two instead of all at once, and lure the TIE fighters away from the drops with the other bombers.

Their plan went perfectly. They were able to complete the second drop, with the TIE fighters thoroughly distracted.

Now there were only two drops to go.

But on their way back to the base to reload for the next run, a terrible shock tore through the fabric of space.

The Resistance ships were okay, but nobody could figure out where the violent disturbance had come from.

Rose and Paige had never felt anything like it, but they tried to shake the odd jolt from their minds. Their squadron had two final supply runs to finish and the First Order to contend with.

But strangely enough, the First Order didn't show up when the Resistance bombers made their next supply run *or* during their fourth and final drop.

There were no TIE fighters and no battles. There was just empty space and the feeling in Rose's gut that something wasn't right.

"It's as if . . ." she started.

"As if the First Order thinks they have a weapon so big they don't need to worry about a few heavy bombers?" Paige replied.

They had both heard rumors that the First Order was working on a weapon that dwarfed the Death Star itself.

Rose shuddered.

The squadron returned to base. They had successfully completed their mission, but General Organa's second-in-command, Vice Admiral Holdo, was waiting for them.

She explained that the shock they had all felt ripple through space was a First Order attack that had destroyed the Hosnian system, the location of the New Republic's capital.

Without the New Republic, there was only the First Order and the Resistance—and war.

Vice Admiral Holdo turned to Rose. "I need you on my ship."

Rose looked to her sister. This would be the first time they had ever been apart.

My sister is the most important thing in the world to me, Rose thought as she clutched Paige's hand. Paige squeezed back encouragingly.

But defeating the First Order is the most important thing in the galaxy.

Rose and Paige nodded to each other. They would follow Holdo—and Leia—into battle.

The Resistance needed them.

The galaxy needed them.

It was their destiny to help defeat the First Order.